D0880547

*Mistress of*
# REDEMPTION
# JOEY W. HILL

ELLORA'S CAVE
ROMANTICA PUBLISHING

# *What the critics are saying...*

ॐ

"Ms. Hill is definitely an auto-buy author for this reviewer! MISTRESS OF REDEMPTION is keeper that you really don't want to miss." ~ *Love Romances and More*

"Joey W. Hill has this ability to create rich, round characters who are so complex that they may as well be living! This story is heart wrenching and absolutely beautiful."
~ *ECataromance*

"*Mistress of Redemption* is the story of two very broken souls who find salvation, redemption, and their other halves in the acceptance and forgiveness of one another. Joey W. Hill did a great job of writing this interesting and disturbing tale."
~ *Two Lips Reviews*

"As always, Ms. Hill tells a gripping story that draws forth an honest emotional response. I must also mention the sex scenes as they are blazing hot and worth rereading many times. I highly recommend *Mistress of Redemption* to anyone looking for a truly fabulous story of love and BDSM." ~ *Coffee Time Romance*

"Not only is Ms. Hill an artist with words, but she also continues to display a true talent for showcasing phenomenal character development." ~ *Fallen Angel Reviews*

An Ellora's Cave Romantica Publication

www.ellorascave.com

Mistress of Redemption

ISBN 9781419959516
ALL RIGHTS RESERVED.
Mistress of Redemption Copyright © 2006 Joey W. Hill
Edited by Briana St. James.
Cover art by Syneca & Willo.

This book printed in the U.S.A. by Jasmine-Jade Enterprises, LLC.

Electronic book Publication September 2006
Trade paperback Publication July 2009

With the exception of quotes used in reviews, this book may not be reproduced or used in whole or in part by any means existing without written permission from the publisher, Ellora's Cave Publishing, Inc.® 1056 Home Avenue, Akron OH 44310-3502.

Warning: The unauthorized reproduction or distribution of this copyrighted work is illegal. Criminal copyright infringement, including infringement without monetary gain, is investigated by the FBI and is punishable by up to 5 years in federal prison and a fine of $250,000.
(http://www.fbi.gov/ipr/)

This book is a work of fiction and any resemblance to persons, living or dead, or places, events or locales is purely coincidental. The characters are productions of the author's imagination and used fictitiously.

# MISTRESS OF
# REDEMPTION

෨

For those of you familiar with my earlier works, *Holding the Cards* and *Natural Law*, the idea that Jonathan is getting his own story might be shocking. Make a hero out of the "bad guy" who nearly destroyed Lauren's soul? Who almost got Mac killed? Joey, have you lost your mind?!

Jonathan was the worst kind of bottom. A twisted sub, a sexual predator who enjoyed manipulative games with his chosen Mistresses until he destroyed them emotionally and moved on to his next prey. The only person who stopped him was a Mistress who was more of a sociopath than he was, who used him to try to kill Mac Nighthorse. If she had succeeded, of course my fans would have wanted to consign Jonathan to Hell forever, for no male hero of mine to date has been as widely beloved as Mac Nighthorse of *Natural Law*.

Truth be told, it never occurred to me that Jonathan should have his own story. Not until a fan (who is a Domme) started pushing me in that direction with questions like "Why does he continually have to prove his manhood by submitting and then manipulating others? How does it serve him better than being a regular Dom or a bottom? Why choose to masquerade as a sub? Deep down, is he a real sub? What does he get out of it? What would it take to stop him in his tracks and make him see what he's missing by never surrendering himself to real intimacy? What would force the issue, breach those walls?"

Just like that, Mistress Dona appeared in my imagination and I knew that Jonathan needed her. What cinched it was finding out how much she needed *him*. When two people are bound the way these two were, I have to write their story. So here's *Mistress of Redemption*. I won't say enjoy the journey, because it's not that kind of trip, but I hope you find something here that feeds your heart and soul.

This book is dedicated to "Maven", who believed enough in Jonathan that she convinced me and my Muse to look deeper. To believe that even the worst among us might be redeemed, if the love and justice applied is strong and balanced enough to heal the soul. It makes me wish there were more Donas in the world, people able to drive evil away and help the soul find its way back to the gift of unconditional love freely offered by another.

Joey W. Hill

# Trademarks Acknowledgement

ℰↃ

The author acknowledges the trademarked status and trademark owners of the following wordmarks mentioned in this work of fiction:

Aerosmith: Rag Doll Merchandising, Inc.

Band-Aids: Johnson & Johnson Corporation

*GQ*: Conde Nast Publications Inc.

Kahlua: The Kahlua Company

Mercedes: DaimlerChrysler AG Corporation

Monopoly: Hasbro, Inc.

Play-Doh: General Mills Fun Group, Inc.

Superman: National Comics Publications, Inc.

# Chapter One

**ᔓ**

The duffel bag hit the edge of the road, sending up a puff of gravel dust that lingered, seemingly reluctant to settle in the still, humid air. The day he'd been brought to Wentworth Prison it had been hot and sticky, for Florida summers knew no other way to be, but it had not been like this. The light of the sun was harsh, painful to the eyes as it reflected on a ribbon of asphalt flanked by expanses of sand and scrub that stretched out from one horizon to another. He hadn't remembered the prison being the only feature of this desolate wasteland, but five years was a long time to remember a detail that had been so insignificant at the time.

He could have moved back into the shadow of the guard tower to wait for the bus, but he rejected the idea. He wasn't planning on turning around or looking at the prison ever again.

Prisoners about to be released had two choices for transport. He could catch a bus ride back to the county in which he was arrested, compliments of the state, or he could make his own pickup arrangements. Call a friend, a family member.

So he waited for the bus, not because he had any interest in going back to Tampa, but because there was no one to call. The life he'd built for himself—Jonathan Powell, successful stockbroker, upwardly mobile twenty-something—was over. Gone and ill-fitting on him now, like a costume the day after Halloween. He had enough to live on for a while, but his old employer wouldn't be begging to have him back. Not the accomplice to the S&M Killer, the woman who'd tried to off two cops as her final coup. He wouldn't find a career in

11

finance, where corporations regularly did criminal background checks as part of the hiring process.

It didn't matter. He'd find a hotel, a shower and plan to be across the country in a week. Maybe Oregon. Mountains. Cool, green. He could hire himself out as a subcontractor in places where new construction was booming. Once, in another life, he'd been a better-than-decent roofer. Fearless no matter the pitch, always keeping his balance. Sometimes he'd taken his lunch break up there. Sitting shirtless in loose jeans, his knees drawn up to anchor himself on the slope as he ate his sandwich, he'd almost felt at peace. Clean despite the filth that had dried in a film on his sun-browned skin from the hot, dirty work.

A loser, he reminded himself. He'd been a no-money, nobody loser then. And here he was again.

When a wavering line appeared on the horizon, he squinted. Sweat rolled down the center of his back and dampened the waistband of his jeans. Damn bus probably wouldn't be air-conditioned, just a fan up front for the driver.

It wasn't a bus. It was a car. A red Mercedes convertible, the top down, the driver flying along at what looked to be a smooth ninety. The exhaust turned the air around the car into a mirage, wavy lines confusing the eyes so reality vied with illusion. Then the car drew closer, became more defined. As did the driver.

A woman. A woman with dark sunglasses, red lips and dark hair whipping and tangling around her face. He could almost feel the pleasure of the wind as he stood in stagnant heat. The idea of seeing a real woman, even if it was just a flash as she passed him on this godforsaken highway, curled its way around his cock and stroked it like the touch of her fingers. With long, wicked nails that might dig into tender flesh just a little. Taking a drag on his cigarette, he savored the vision and waited.

A hundred yards away, she hit the brakes. Hard. Turned the wheel directly for him. The car screamed its fury as a ripple of flame shot out beneath the back tire treads, an impressive pyrotechnic display.

Before he could get a curse out, the car had come to a snorting, quivering halt, blowing hot air and dust across his groin and thighs.

Lifting the cigarette deliberately back to his lips, he took another drag. Held it there a moment so he wouldn't betray a tremor in his fingers. Son of a bitch, he hadn't expected that.

He still cared about being alive.

"You trolling for prison dick, Princess?"

One slim brow rose and then so did she, performing a sinuous wriggle to stand up on the cushioned seat of the Mercedes and prop her hips against the headrest.

His cock was going to get hard at any hint of pussy, never mind the feast she was displaying in front of him now. He'd have turned around to see if the guards were falling out of the tower, if he gave a rat's ass. Or if he didn't prefer the territory his eyes were covering right now just fine.

Despite the heat that was making his cotton clothes feel like impermeable raingear, this bitch was wearing a black corset, laced so tight his hands would have spanned her waist easily. What was spilling out of the top was much harder to contain. Jayne Mansfield tits, the kind that could suffocate a man and make him die happy. The latex pants were painted on, the thigh-high boots covering them having the effect of zeroing his attention on her crotch, the lips of her cunt distinct and separate under the provocative creases.

When he raised his gaze to her face, he found those lips were indeed red, full and wet. Ready to suck a man's cock and leave him marked with her makeup like traces of blood. Her eyes were rimmed with black, her lashes thick, completing the Goth look of her attire. A triple-looped chain of silver sunbursts and crescent moon metal discs rode low on her hips, calling attention to the way they cocked against the headrest. She wore gloves up to her elbows. The only flesh visible below her face was her upper arms, the rounded curves of her shoulders, the line of her throat and slim jaw. Plus that tempting valley of cleavage.

"The only dick I'm trolling for is yours, Nathan."

His gaze snapped up, focused more intently on her face. "Dona?"

She inclined her head. "You've a good memory."

"Not as good as yours, if you're here on my release date."

Not expecting to see a familiar face today, he hadn't bothered to look past the display of high-grade pussy. Now he couldn't believe he hadn't recognized her right off, but then she would have tied with a complete stranger as the last person he'd have anticipated showing up for him.

At The Zone, the fetish club she most frequented, she'd had a reputation for being a supreme bitch of a Mistress, able to bring a man to his knees and make him beg for anything. He'd never been able to get this close to her. The few times his gaze had found her through the dim light of the club, she'd been studying him, her dark eyes unreadable. When he'd been in a savage enough mood to try and fuck with the mind of a hard-core Mistress like her, she'd been nowhere to be found. His curiosity had driven him to seek out more information about her. Strangely enough, despite her renown, no one could identify a man who'd served her. No one had been able to offer a firsthand account so he could learn her technique. Her weaknesses.

He dropped the cigarette, ground it out and hooked his thumbs in his belt loops, curling his fingers loosely on his thighs on either side of his crotch.

"So if you're here for my dick, spread yourself on the hood of that Mercedes, baby. I'll be happy to do you right here."

She didn't bat an eyelash, but her gaze coursed smoothly over him, lingering on his groin. "You always were blessed in that area. A nice, thick tool to make a Mistress sigh with pleasure. You had a good body. But prison used those muscles, made them real, didn't it? It toughened you up good. I like your hair longer, that dangerous glint to those pretty blue eyes. You're looking like a fine, cool drink of water out here in the hot desert. I've a mind to take you somewhere I can enjoy that tool and those muscles at my own pace."

Her tone was as sultry as the weather. Her eyes, as they lifted back to his, were as relentless as the sun's heat. He knew she wasn't inviting him anywhere. Her manner said that if he knew what was good for him, he'd get his ass in the car.

"I'm out of that now."

"Yeah." Those lips curved in a mocking smile, her attention dropping back down to his erection pressing against his jeans, a reaction he'd indifferently made more noticeable by the frame of his large hands on either side of it. "I can see that."

"I've seen nothing but ugly bastards with dicks for five years, and you've driven up in an outfit that says you're here to give me some. So stop being a cock-tease and offer it. Or fuck off." He patted his shirt for another cigarette.

"Oh, you're pushing it, sweet boy. Just begging for punishment, aren't you?"

His fingers fumbled the pack the moment she said it, a trigger inside him squeezing off, making him even harder. He clamped down on the cigarette with his teeth. Feeling in the narrow confines of a jeans pocket for his lighter, he found he couldn't get his fingers down there, his organ had gotten so huge.

"Come here." She crooked a finger at him. It sported a long black glossy nail with a silver star appliqué that flashed, giving the sharp point of the nail the appearance of a scalpel in the glaring sunlight. His lower extremities became even tauter. He was likely going to cream himself just from looking at her.

He didn't like the way she was looking at him. All proprietary, as though he were a dog she knew wasn't content unless he was at a Mistress's heel.

He didn't want to play this game. He'd planned a simple, uncomplicated fuck with a paid whore, followed by that shave and shower. He just needed to get his uncooperative cock to understand that.

"I'm waiting for the bus." The fucking bus that should have been here by now.

"Jonathan Powell, on public transportation." She mocked his gruff tone. "Wouldn't he rather be seen with a sexy woman in a fast, powerful car? I've already set up an appointment for your haircut and manicure. A full shave." When her attention lowered again, he swore he felt the feathering of those thick lashes stroke his cock from twenty feet away. "Or is he running away because there's a woman he doesn't think he can handle?"

Her words taunted him inside the way her voice was doing outside. He perused her thoroughly, resting his attention insolently long on those luscious tits before he gave her a mocking bow.

"What the hell. For a shower and a shave, I guess I'm all yours, Mistress."

Picking up his bag, he strode to the door of the car on her side and tossed it into the backseat under her intent regard. "Like what you see?"

"I like to study my food before I eat it. It's called savoring, Nathan."

"Jonathan. I go by Jonathan. Someone told you wrong at the club."

"That's not what you call yourself."

Before he could circle around to the passenger side, she bent forward, giving him a view of her breasts that made him want to howl like a ravenous wolf. Reaching out, she slid two fingers deep into the recesses of the pocket of his jeans and found his lighter. She retracted it, making him hyperaware of his hard cock only an inch away from her touch. When she got it free, she fired the lighter in a mean line drive across the road so it landed on the asphalt and clattered off into the sand. Plucking his cigarettes out of his shirt pocket, she tossed them in the same direction. "I'll call you whatever I fucking want. You won't be smoking. You're my slave, so get your ass in the car. *Nathan.*"

The anger surged up in him, hot, bloodthirsty. He made no effort to hide it, narrowing his gaze. It was a look other prisoners had learned to respect. She merely waited, those breasts at eye level, dominating his vision. God, she smelled so...female. Perfume. Hair shampoo. Body spray. Powdery female deodorant. He wanted to wallow in those scents, in a woman. He despised himself for needing one like her far more than he needed a vanilla fuck.

Mistresses knew a submissive man's needs were more complex. He wasn't a complete whipped candy-ass like other male subs. However, he couldn't deny fucking with a Domme's head had taught him pleasure like nothing else had. Her standing there with that "I'm-going-to-work-you-over" smug smile on her face was more than he could resist. So he tried out a smile of his own, one he hadn't pulled out of his hat in over five years. A smile capable of making a woman wet just from the implication of it. "May I help you back down behind the wheel? *Mistress.*"

With an amused look that made him feel as if she was scoffing at him, she placed her hand in his. The feel of a woman's fingers, delicate and smooth, capable of being merciful or merciless, made his hand tighten briefly. While he absorbed his own reaction, she stood still, apparently waiting for his next move, a surprise courtesy. He almost sensed...compassion. As well as a terrible knowledge he didn't have and didn't want to know about himself. It raised a need in him so strong he wouldn't give a name to it. If he hadn't known that jerking back might unbalance her and make her

17

fall on her ass, depriving him of his ride, he would have done it. Instead, he steadied his mind and watched her use his weight as a counterbalance to slide back down into the seat. Withdrawing her hand with a nod, she followed him with that same inscrutable look as he circled to the passenger side and got into the car.

"You owe me cigarettes. And a lighter." He rasped it out of a dry throat.

"No, I don't. By the end of our time together, Nathan, you're going to owe me everything."

# Chapter Two

## ❧

The landscape rocketed by, a blur of sand and sharp vegetation. The wind was a blessing on his face, as was the knowledge that the prison was getting farther and farther away. Freedom. His glance cut to the driver. Of a sort. But at what time in his life had he not had to play the angles? There wasn't any such thing as true freedom, not in this crappy-assed world. The dangerous fantasy was believing there could be. A man could give in, delude himself into thinking he could find a substitute for freedom by chaining himself to someone else. He'd found something that gave him a taste of both, a way to be beyond everyone's grasp when they thought he was captured. She'd be no different. He told himself he'd enjoy the game, particularly with this one. Like the taste of an ice-cold beer after years of nothing but tepid water.

He could be called crazy for even getting into her car. His last such relationship was what had landed him in prison. However, he'd had time to think it over from every angle and he knew what his mistake had been in that situation. He'd let his hatred of another male submissive, Mac Nighthorse, blind him to the dangers of the Mistress who had offered him the opportunity to even the score. Too late he'd learned that Nighthorse was a homicide detective and Jonathan's Mistress of the moment had cleverly used him in a plan of attempted murder. He wouldn't let his emotions make him stupid again. If he could get some cushy spa service and maybe a soft hotel bed for playing slave boy for a few hours, no skin off his back. His lips twisted. Unless this Mistress was into flogging.

It didn't matter. His hard-on hadn't eased up one bit and he ached for release. He hadn't jacked himself off in prison, not even once. Something no other prisoner in that place could claim, he was sure. Even most of the guards. So there certainly wasn't any harm in letting his fingers drift across the console onto her thigh. The frustratingly snug, impenetrable latex denied him the sense of the skin beneath.

She caught two of his fingers and wrenched them backward, sending searing pain through his palm and wrist. "Ow. *Jesus...*" The angle was perfect. He couldn't pull away, couldn't move in any direction without causing himself more agony. "Let go."

"Did I give you permission to touch me?"

Her voice was cool. She wasn't even taking her eyes off the road and damn if that very aloofness wasn't arousing him further. When she tightened her grip, he hissed.

"I don't play cutesy with my slaves. They give me absolute obedience or they're punished. Severely."

"This isn't a dungeon, sweetheart. D/s is just a game. Can we get to where we're going before you slip into playing—"

His voice climbed two octaves as she twisted her grip. He was sure he felt his bones begin to crack. If he brought his other hand across his body, he wasn't so certain she wouldn't snap one. "Jesus, let me go."

"This is not a game. It never has been to you. It's not to me. Ask for my forgiveness or you'll have two fingers permanently curved backward to hit my sweet spot when I give you permission to put them into my pussy. Say it."

"My apologies, Mistress. I'm sorry."

Though he spat it out, apparently it was enough. She released him, as unflappable as she'd been before she'd tried to make his fingers bend a hundred and eighty degrees in the wrong direction. He rubbed his hand, eyed her profile. The hourglass design of her body in that corset, the curve of her hips, the way her buttocks pressed into the seat, even how she pushed down on the gas with the sole of the three-inch spike heel, made him both resent her and want her all the more. The dark waves of her hair whispered around her face as she drove, but now he could see that the mass of it was pinned on her head, making him wonder how long and thick it was, what it would look like spilled over her bare body. Closing his eyes, he turned his face away. It *had* been a mistake to get into the car.

"Let me set out the rules for you up front. You won't charm me or play with my emotions," she said. "I'm not interested in that. I want your pain, your suffering. I want your fear." When he glanced back at her warily, she was looking straight at him. "I'm the Goddess of the Old Testament, Jonathan. You're not going to crawl into a crack in my psyche. You serve me, not the other way around. Everything about you is dependent upon your Mistress's Will."

Then he felt her hand on his thigh, sliding over it to cup him. Without any conscious thought or command from his brain, his hips pushed up eagerly into her touch, the stroke and pinch of her fingertips.

"Nice," she purred. "Take it out. I want to play with it while I drive." Her lips moved into a pout that caused his attention to fasten hungrily on her mouth. "They didn't have this car in anything but automatic and I like to move a stick when I drive." Her brown eyes were like that of a she-wolf considering prey. "That was a command. Or have you forgotten your body is your Mistress's toy?"

He found his hands moving to the button of his jeans, working it open and jerking the zipper down in the same motion.

"Take the jeans and underwear off. I want that fine ass bare against the seat."

It wasn't self-consciousness that gave him a brief hesitation. There was no one out here and he could always snatch up his clothes if needed. Having performed as a submissive countless times before, Nathan didn't balk at modesty. He was concerned about the fact that his cock was so rigid with lust he might spew at the touch of his own hand. Regardless, he obeyed. The burn of the hot upholstery on his ass helped distract him. He took some small satisfaction in the flare of appreciation in her gaze as he revealed himself to her. She did feel something, which meant she could be made to feel more. Tossing his boots in the back, he left his clothes in a heap at his feet. Strategy vanished as she closed her hand over him, a firm, commanding grip tugging on him. "Over here."

Her fingers caressed him in sensual torture as he gingerly slid his leg over the center console, avoiding the gearshift. When he placed his now bare foot in the narrow space beside her heel where she pressed down on the gas, his arm stretched around the back of her seat. With his fingers gripped in the cushioning, he could feel her whipping hair caress his fingertips, resting only an inch or so away from her shoulder. It was an awkward position for a tall man, but he didn't care as she laid her forearm on his bare thigh and took hold of him again as if his cock were a manual stick in truth, fondling him as he braced his other leg in the passenger side. Keeping his ass firmly pressed back against the opening between the two seats, he hoped he wouldn't lose control and jerk forward, knocking the car out of gear. They had climbed to ninety-five, the landscape a blur, the wind a roar she'd had to raise her voice over to issue the command. The whip of the wind on his bare lower body intertwined with her touch to twist the hard spear of want piercing his lower belly. It gave him a peculiar sense of sensual freedom, the desire to lay his head back, close his eyes and feel the wind rush over him as her touch took him soaring.

However, because the position put him above her, he had a throat-clogging view of her breasts in the corset, the full crescent shape of the globes of flesh molded by the fabric. The vibration of the Mercedes made them quiver. If he strained his eyes, the rise and fall of her breath almost gave him the hint of her nipples. He was straining, in more ways than one.

She took control of his reaction as if his cock were in fact connected to the transmission of the car, engine revving for her, eager to be put into drive. Her thumb caressed his broad head, collecting his pre-cum on the end of one of those glossy nails.

He had to look away or he'd explode. In contrast, she drove with the same calm demeanor, her hand touching his dick as casually and maddeningly as if she were merely entertaining herself with the feel of an inanimate gearshift beneath her palm, something for her free hand to do as she drove one-handed.

In that outfit, he couldn't tell if her nipples were getting hard or her pussy wet, while his body was reacting almost violently to her indifferent use of him. He knew it was a Mistress's right to use a slave in such a cavalier fashion, but it infuriated him, her impassive behavior.

Patience. He wanted to roar it to his subconscious, but it was more like a hoarse plea for attention. His fingers dug into the side of the seat as that thumb rocked back and forth over him, tracing the helmet shape of the head, curving under to follow the flare at the base and then... Oh, God, now she was on that vein on the underside that was throbbing, begging for some kind of consistent stroke or rhythm. He wanted to pump into her hand, jerk himself off viciously, but he couldn't move without disrupting the vehicle. The automatic gearshift was a mere inch from his balls, almost pressing into them. Her nails were touching the top of it as she caressed him.

Plus, she hadn't given him permission to move. Jonathan Powell had always been the perfect sub, everything a Mistress could ask him to be. That was key. He had to remember that now, be what she expected him to be so he could get the upper hand. It would have been easier if he'd had time to fuck some willing hooker, take that shower and put his veneer into place, but he'd learned to think on his feet in prison. This was no different. He just needed to get it together, get past his hormones.

"Ah, here we are." She slowed the car, turned off the highway. Startled, he realized he had zoned out on his surroundings to the point that he had missed the change in the landscape.

He'd found the empty terrain of desert and scrub curious when he'd come out of the prison, for he hadn't remembered it that way. Now his confusion increased as it yielded to an oasis. A mirage like something out of *Arabian Nights*. As they wound down the road, sand and desolation became palm trees, lush green grass and some kind of man-made lagoon, so clear that it mirrored the blue sky above.

There were women here. He blinked as he saw a long-legged, tawny-skinned creature with hair past her buttocks ambling with the sway of a pendulum by the water's edge. A leopard twined around her calves, bumping her hand to make her stroke the spotted head.

Naked. The woman was completely naked and... As she turned, he thought the sun showed her dusky skin marked with a faint pattern like the leopard. Even more startling, when her lips curved, tiny sharp canines glittered just over her full bottom lip.

Two other women lounged on the green grass of the banks. One was asleep. The other, a blonde, was stroking the napping one's red hair and braiding it into tiny tails, just the tip ends so the mass of it remained loose and thick on her pale shoulders. Shoulders seemingly unaffected by the bright sunlight. Another trio of women played some type of game under the palm trees. His eyes widened. The game apparently involved the playful teasing of a cobra. The snake rose up to take a scrap of meat from one woman's fingers as she crooned to it, while the other women played with its coils. It paid no attention to them in favor of the treat.

"Did I... I'm dreaming."

"You may have nodded off for a little while," Dona agreed. He realized then his boots and jeans were back on, though he wasn't wearing the scratchy prison underwear anymore. He was back in his seat, though he didn't remember moving or arranging his clothes. No more than he remembered taking his shirt off, though now her hand was on his shoulder, caressing his bare skin. She'd had hold of his cock, he'd been on the edge of explosion and he'd nodded off? *What the hell…*

She parked the car on a patch of green under one of the palms. Reaching over again, she ran her hand down his chest and caressed the indentation of his navel, her other fingers playing over his sectioned stomach. "So how many times did your fine ass and pretty face get you raped before you learned how to use these muscles?"

"It doesn't matter. Once you teach them it won't happen without someone dying or walking away maimed, the past doesn't matter."

"So why didn't you charm or manipulate them like you try to do your Mistresses? Why did you fight them, every time?"

He was too confounded by the change in landscape to get his mind around how she would know all of that. He knew the answer to the question, though. Because no one was taking what he wasn't willing to give. Even if it was just a response to a question. So he just shrugged.

"What is this place?"

"This is one of my favorite playgrounds. Come. Get out and leave the shirt. This is where we'll get you cleaned up."

When he got out, he looked back at the dusty road, the ribbon of highway now farther in the distance than he remembered the drive to the oasis being. A deserted highway on which there'd not been a single car other than hers. The Mercedes was the only vehicle here as well, despite the presence of the other women. "Is this far from the prison?"

"Very far. Or not far at all, depending on your perspective." When she walked across the grass, he was forced to follow if he wanted to continue the dialogue. He was amazed at how easily she walked in those high heels. With a sauntering stride, her ass twitching left and right in a way

designed to make him not really give a damn about the
unlikely nature of their surroundings or the lack of logic to
them. He'd sworn to make no more mistakes like the one that
had landed him in prison, though. Self-preservation had to be
his first priority in any situation. "Dona. *Where are we?*"

She stopped but kept her back to him. The breeze
fluttered through her hair as she turned her head, just enough
for him to see her profile, the red lips, dark eyes and lashes
lowered over them behind the sunglasses.

"This is part of my home. One small part of it."

The wind died. Clouds closed in on the sun so abruptly it
was as if a curtain had been drawn over it by human hands, a
curtain that couldn't shut out an ominous rumble like thunder.

"It *is* my home." She repeated it, almost a snarl.
Fascinated, he saw her fingers close into clenched fists at her
sides, her chin thrust up in defiance.

A blink and abruptly the sun was out again, the curtain
drawn away as if it had never been there. The six women, who
had gone still at that rumble, resumed their movement and
idle play. The wind gusted through the palm fronds then
settled back to a mild breeze, as if someone had sighed.

Giving a slight nod, apparently satisfied, Dona looked
back at him. "I told you to come with me. Why are you way
back there? Have you forgotten how to obey a Mistress as
well?"

This was all tipping the bizarre meter, enough to make
him think he'd be better off heading back to the highway and
hitching to the seedy hotel he'd intended for his first night. But
maybe the heat had gotten to him. He'd stood out in front of
the prison for a while, hadn't he? If this was just a part of her
home, Dona had to be loaded. Mega wealthy. Why should he
be afraid of her? In prison, he'd gotten used to anticipating the
less subtle reactions of men. It was time to sharpen the
instincts that he'd once kept honed to surgical precision to pick
up on a woman's deepest needs and fears. She'd just

demonstrated that there was something that could get under her skin. He needed to push aside the lingering self-doubt caused by the nearly fatal mistake he'd made with his last Mistress. He'd learned since then. He wouldn't make the same mistakes, miss the cues he'd missed with her.

Sweeping his lashes down, he took the first true step away from his current existence and back toward Jonathan Powell, the polished blue-eyed, blond-haired Norse god that so many women had eyed with covetous appreciation at The Zone, True Blue and the other BDSM clubs he'd frequented. Only this version would be new and improved. Way smarter. "My apologies, Mistress," he murmured. "I don't feel well-groomed enough to serve your needs properly. You deserve a slave who has shaved and showered."

"Yes, I do. I'll attend to those things. Your only job is to obey me. Take off your clothes again."

At the order, the three women playing with the cobra stopped. The napping woman woke up and the leopard woman turned to watch, her golden eyes narrowed in the exact same expression as the great cat who took a seat on the grass next to her while the water lapped at the woman's bare ankles. For some reason, it brought to mind the Waterhouse painting of the nymphs coming out of the water to drag Hylas to his death with the promise of pleasure. Anxiety settled low in his belly. This was a fear that could not be countered with violence. Somehow he'd felt less isolated among men who might kill or beat him unmercifully for the barest transgression than he felt among all these attentive women.

"Too long, Jonathan. You need a reminder."

Dona was upon him before he knew it. Even as he spun in surprised reaction, her arm swept forward. Suddenly there were... It must have been knives she pulled out from a hidden sheath in the back waistband of those painted-on pants, for it couldn't be what he thought he saw. Her fingernails elongating into talons, slicing the waistband of his jeans like silk before a sword blade. The garment fell from him, slit on both sides from the waist to just above the kneecaps. When she drew back to go lower, he hastily shucked them, taking them to his ankles and stumbling, falling onto his ass as he encountered the obstruction of his boots.

She stood over him, her hands on her hips. The weapon, for surely it was a weapon she'd used more quickly than his eyes could follow, was gone. Tucked back into her waistband, perhaps. Fear was ice in his belly when she smiled, her gaze traveling over his naked body.

"Much better. Get the rest off. Now."

He fumbled off the boots, managed to free himself of the pants around his ankles, as much to give himself mobility as to obey. Scrambling to his feet, he backed away from her several steps because she'd stayed right over him, that soft woman's scent at odds with the brutal force she'd just used. Looking down, he saw light scorings on his thighs that looked a lot like fingernails. He'd been marked by enough women's nails to know. But that was impossible.

"I think… Maybe I need some water."

"You need what I tell you to need."

"You're not…" He didn't know why asking would make any difference, considering he was out in the middle of nowhere and she had the car keys. Maybe he shouldn't ask her the question, because if he did he'd reveal that he suspected something more than a little edge play.

"No, I'm not connected to any of the women whose lives you ruined. I'm not here to exercise revenge on you."

A relief to hear, but what the fuck? Ruined? *Who's the one that just got out of prison because I got fucked over by a woman, bitch?*

"Sshh. Be quiet. Look at me."

He hadn't spoken aloud. He was sure he hadn't. Taking a step closer, she put her hand to his jaw and tilted her face up so she was looking directly into his startled eyes.

"No, I can't read your mind. I just read faces very well. I've had more practice than you can imagine. I know a great deal about you, Jonathan."

Though he grudgingly admitted her act was as intimidating as hell, she really was a little thing, more noticeable when she stood this close. Even in the heels, the top of her head would only brush the bottom of his nose. Fear of her motives dropped back a little at her touch, letting him get lost in the liquid depths of those brown eyes, the ebony pupils. How could she be so frightening and yet make him think of a deer moving through the shadowed glades of a forest? An elusive and delicate creature, something worth holding himself still to see how long she'd linger and let him share in the magic of her presence.

"Deep breath. One. Two. Make everything silent, inside and out."

The look in those eyes pierced him like a needle. Though his erection was back up over his balls like an eager dog sitting on his haunches, her hypnotic words drew a thread through his heart and into an even deeper part of himself. A place a much less cynical mind would have called his soul. Dragged it toward her, made him want to do whatever she wanted.

Nathan jerked back from her touch. "What the hell are you doing?"

Moving right with him, she insinuated her thigh between his, against the bulge of his testicles. She put her palm close to his mouth. "Taste me and you won't fear me for the wrong reasons. Or are you too afraid already?"

He managed a sneer that he realized was not the type of expression that charmed a wealthy Mistress. So slowly, keeping his gaze on her face, he dipped his head, pressed his lips to her palm and tasted soft skin. The pads of her fingers brushed his brow. They were cool and he felt…peace. Closing his eyes, he leaned into her touch, his throat tight with a wealth of emotions, needs and desires so overwhelming that all he could do was be still and let them roll through him. He obeyed her, stilling all thought and motion, inhaling her scent with flared nostrils, willing away any other distraction.

"There you go. That's my good boy. My handsome slave."

Fingers brushed his cock and his breath shuddered out of him. When a strap tightened on the root, his eyes snapped open. Dona still stood before him, but the previously napping redhead knelt at her hip, buckling a cock strap on him. He tried to pull back but he was already caught, the stiff collar digging into the base of his cock and testicles. It was snug enough it didn't need a waist strap, especially now with his dick swelling up large, as it always had when a woman restrained him. He used to think it was a curse, until he learned how to twist it for his own purposes. It didn't escape his notice, however, that the only thing apparently being twisted at the moment was him.

The woman who'd been braiding the hair of the redhead, the blonde with the requisite cornflower blue eyes and pale pink lips that were curved in a pleased smile, handed Dona a metal collar with a padlock.

"No—"

The blonde moved behind him and caught his arms, drawing the wrists back. When he began to struggle in earnest, the redhead neatly pulled his legs out from under him. He should have been able to easily overpower both, but the swift attack took him unawares. Rolling him over onto his stiff cock caused him to yelp, but they held him fast as Dona straddled his back, her ass on his neck, those slim ankles in spiked heels on either side of his head. Bending his arms, she manacled his wrists to his elbows so his arms were folded at a ninety-degree angle against his back.

Immobilized, he drew in a breath as the blonde caressed his throat and threaded the collar under him so she could snap it on. A chain attached to the manacles was drawn up and clipped to the back of the collar so that the weight of his arms pulled against it. When he heard the padlock click, felt the pressure of the metal against his throat, his balls drew up hard and tight, sending a spurt of his fluids into the grass, making him groan.

"You like that," his new Mistress observed. "You like the feeling of being owned, though you hate it in yourself as well. Always trying to pretend it's something else, something you can use to your advantage."

Dona bent forward, her breasts pressing against the small of his back, her abdomen in the stiff corset brushing against the upper curve of his spine between his shoulders. He pushed against the ground when she touched his buttock with the tip of her tongue, tasted him with sharp teeth, bit into the meat of his left cheek. His cock, uncomfortably mashed against the ground, hardened further. All he could think about was that tight ass and those thighs on either side of his head, wondering what it would be like to turn over on his back and take a taste between them.

Why not? He *was* stronger than three women, though of course they'd now stacked things in their favor by restraining him. He flipped over, using those muscles Dona had admired and caressed. While he jerked the other women loose with the motion, he made the turn without dislodging Dona. It seemed his Mistress was experienced at riding broncs. It put his face within access of that pussy, encased in impervious material though it was. *Let's see if she's impervious to this.* He reared up, only to snarl in frustration when he found there was no slack in the chain between the back of his collar and folded arms. He couldn't rise to the proper angle without strangling himself. For a moment it didn't matter. He was like a dog with the scent of a bitch in his nose, his desire desperate. He kept pulling until the lack of oxygen penetrated the haze of lust enough to make him notice that by tightening her thighs incremental amounts she was keeping just out of reach, taunting him.

"Beg for it, Jonathan." Her lips moved on his upper thigh, her tongue playing along the crease between it and his hip.

The women had moved away as if Dona had waved them off, so she controlled him with nothing more than her seductive voice and the brush of her cheek along his ball sac and cock, a steel shuttle awaiting launch.

He'd lose nothing by begging. Mistresses got soft when you begged. So why was he finding it hard to obey, as if he was losing ground where he hadn't even gained any yet? It tore out of him roughly, like a scab pulled off an unhealed wound. "Please, Mistress. Let me taste you."

When she moved back into him, her ass pressed against his face, the curves of her buttocks against his nose. The lips of her cunt were frustratingly beyond his reach behind her latex, but they were there. So he closed his mouth over the stiff fabric, tracing her with his tongue, using his teeth for pressure, wishing she'd worn something more flimsy so he could rip it away, play his tongue over her. Feel her body draw tight along the length of his as he did it. He knew he could make her thighs clamp down harder on his head, her breath pant hot and fast on his cock as she came.

"Dona." A sultry voice broke through his wishful thinking and the rasp of his breath. When Dona shifted, he saw the leopard woman stood at his ankles. Her pubic hair was a smooth short pelt of gold, her breasts solid and tempting as grapefruit. Squatting, she ran a hand over Dona's hair, then reached down and snapped a tether on his cock harness, giving it a sharp yank so he jumped. "Let us prepare him for you. He's still coated in the filth of that place. I could smell his prison stench the moment you drove up." She wrinkled her nose.

"She's not complaining," he growled before he could stop himself. The woman's gaze rose to him and he saw she had diamond-shaped pupils in the bright light. Her lip curled up to show her canines, the overall impression so eerily like a cat it made his blood run a few degrees cooler, despite all the body modifications he logically knew were out there now. Sharpened teeth, split tongues...

Rising off him in one fluid movement, Dona stood over him, looking down the length of his body while he stared up at her. His cock throbbed, his mouth salivating for more, for anything she was willing to give him. His shoulders and arms ached from the discomfort of lying on them. At the moment all her expression was giving him was indifference, making him wonder if he'd imagined her thighs quiver as he tongued her, the wiggle of her ass against his face, the clutch of her fingers on his thighs.

"Thank you, Fiona. Take him."

Fiona nodded. Jerking her head at Nathan, she underscored Dona's desire with another sharp tug. He had a momentary thought to raise his foot and boot her back on her ass. Except the bitch likely would hang on to the harness and tear his dick off.

Fiona's lips curved as if she sensed his dour thoughts. "On your feet, slave. We're taking you down to the water."

# Chapter Three

§C

As he struggled to his feet, Dona pivoted and walked away without another glance at him. When her arms rose to loosen her hair, it tumbled down her back in a way that made him lose track of time. The ends whispered along the sleek black pants that defined the curves of her ass.

Before he could linger on the image, his upper arms were taken on either side by the redhead and the blonde, their nails biting into his biceps as they got him to his feet. Fiona led the way down to the water. With trepidation, he saw the three who had played with the cobra headed their way. The snake was wound around the arm and looped low on the bare hips of a woman with smooth chocolate skin and dark eyes like Dona's, only hers had crimson lashes and the brown irises reflected red in the sunlight. Her large breasts were a convenient platform for another of the cobra's coils, his head resting on her shoulder almost like a baby's, his flickering tongue occasionally brushing her earlobe.

"The snake isn't coming into the water with us, is it?" He balked, despite himself. Before Fiona could yank on him again, the redhead's cool fingers slipped between his buttocks, teasing his anus, making him lunge into forward motion again.

"He's jumpy and tight, Fiona. You'll like that."

Fiona sent a wicked look over her shoulder and Nathan curled his lip at her in a snarl. *In your dreams, bitch.* Though even as he had the thought, he knew it might be desperate bravado, for he wasn't able to prevent them from doing much in his current situation.

He could bide his time. In prison, he'd sacrificed the necessary pound of flesh to the men who wanted him. While he'd toughened up his muscles as Dona had noted, he quickly learned that becoming stronger and faster would not save him from being outnumbered. He was too good-looking. Too obviously polished and condescending. They thought they were giving him a comeuppance. He was grimly amused they couldn't see through the façade any more than the outside world had. So he taught them the same lesson he'd taught countless others who thought they had the upper hand on him.

Every person could be blindsided with his or her weaknesses. With guile, stealth and the tenacity of a bulldog, he proved he was willing to go to great lengths to stage revenge on those who tortured him. No matter how often he was beaten or raped, he made sure the perpetrator suffered more, whether he did it by planting the right lies to ensure his tormentor was knifed by another inmate, or was sent to Solitary for an infraction he didn't commit. Or maybe the prisoner in question was given the wrong information about his visiting privileges so he missed his opportunity to see a girlfriend or visiting offspring for another long week.

On top of all that, when Jonathan's muscles got tough enough, taking him down had become much, much harder. He'd grin through the blood on his face when the guards caught him and took him for *his* stint in Solitary, never showing the clutch in the pit of his gut at the thought of them closing the door with its one small window, leaving him with four close walls and the sound of their feet walking away.

Things like that didn't matter. What did matter was that he earned the gift of hatred instead of contempt, incurring a grudging respect that was almost gratifying. The attacks had ended after the first year.

When the women pulled him into the water, he sucked in a breath. Despite the fact the oasis had to be in the center of a desert, the water was cold as hell as it sloshed around his calves. Giving him no time to become accustomed to it, they dragged him in to his waist. There'd rarely been a hot shower in prison, but a spray of cold water was not the same as immersion in a vat of it. His nipples beaded up tight, though he noticed the women, all of them naked, were not similarly affected. They seemed as impervious to the frigid temperature as Dona was to the heat in her outfit. Fiona reached out to pinch one of his nubs idly. When he winced and pulled back, they all laughed.

"Mariah, take him under and get his hair wet."

Mariah was apparently the redhead, for she stretched up, wrapped her arms around his neck and shoulders and covered his lips with hers. He yelled his surprise into her open mouth when his feet were yanked out from under him. Hooking one hand on the back of his head, the other pinching his nose, Mariah took him down, his body weighted and held fast by two of the other women.

He struggled despite himself, kicked. His panic increased tenfold when tendrils of something he couldn't immediately identify wound around his ankles. They pulled his legs apart firmly and held him. When his eyes opened and he could see through the wake he was creating, he saw ropes of some kind of pond weed were holding him, though it was hard to make them out past Mariah's flowing hair. Her mouth was wet and hot, her tongue playfully teasing his as his breath rasped hard in and out, his terror making him desperately need oxygen. Thankfully, the women were bringing him up to his feet again, though the organic bindings held his ankles fast, keeping him immobilized for their intentions. As he came up, Mariah let him go and he drew a deep breath, the only one he got before a hard rubber ball gag was shoved in between his teeth and buckled behind his skull, taking another defense away from him. He was starting to shake. The cold, fear and something else were working him, something he couldn't bear to think about. Where was Dona? Where the hell—

He found her standing by the water's edge, watching. She hadn't left him to the mercy of her minions. While he knew this was all being done at her behest, for some reason he clung to that thought as a comfort. The snake woman was sitting on the bank just behind her.

"You're very lucky that Aliyah's pet doesn't like water," Mariah crooned. "She can't resist teasing, particularly when she smells fear. None of us can."

"Olivia, you shave him, we'll wash him." Fiona beckoned to the blonde with a straight-edged razor and Olivia took it. As she approached, Nathan felt Mariah's hands on his dick, unbuckling the harness.

Olivia descended, the blade in her teeth as the waters closed over her head. "I wouldn't move a muscle," Fiona advised. "Ladies, take him back."

"Shit. What the—" The gag muffled the words, underscoring the futility of protesting. While it was a relief to feel the restraints loosen on his ankles, it was a momentary respite, for his calves were seized in the women's hands and he was lifted so he floated horizontally on the water. Now each woman had a portion of him, holding him level. He wanted to thrash as Olivia emerged between his legs, but he believed Fiona's warning. He suspected they could care less if his struggles left him maimed. Olivia slicked back her hair so it clung to her skull as though she were a silver seal touched with gold. She had smaller breasts than Dona, but they curved upward in a tempting manner. A diamond and gold ring glittered at her navel. Removing the razor from her teeth, her gaze lowered to his groin, her tongue coming out to touch her upper lip in anticipation. The cold and fear should have made him as flaccid as a floundering fish, but whether it was the proximity of so many naked women or perhaps his dick had frozen, he was still thick and hard under their greedy eyes.

There were murmurs of appreciation. Giggling, they slapped at his cock as if they were playing a game with the damn snake again. When he tried to duck his hips under the water, an Asian girl with emerald green eyes and hair straight as falling rain put her hand under the water and thrust two fingers up his ass, snapping his spine straight and making him groan with the burning sensation of the non-lubricated entry.

"Be still for Mischa now, slave, or Olivia will turn you into a eunuch," Fiona reproved him. As if he had any control over his body with that almond-eyed siren caressing him deep inside. He managed to focus enough to see Mariah remove the cork from a crystal bottle filled with a green liquid. Tipping the bottle, she drizzled the contents over his navel. As it pooled there and spread out on his abdomen, demonstrating that it was gelatinous and insoluble, the other women used their free hands to rub it across his chest, belly, thighs and arms, making the sticky substance glisten on his muscles. They pinched his nipples, leaned down to nip at his flesh with their mouths.

Olivia moved away and they flipped him, holding him facedown in the water as one of them, probably Mischa, rimmed his ass and rubbed the substance up and down the crease. Even as his panic climbed while they held him where he couldn't breathe, he was sure his cock was leaking pre-cum into the water. The deprivation of air, an extreme BDSM tactic, was goading him. He had to fight the desire to release along with the panic. No way was he giving in to them. Not with his Mistress watching. Though he couldn't see Dona, he could feel her regard, knew she was there.

Just as the terror of being drowned was about to overwhelm him, they flipped him back over. He fought to get air around the gag and not choke on his own saliva, but they were indifferent to his distress. Olivia moved back between his legs to start slicking the razor down his pubic area. Mischa's gel-free hand disappeared back under the water and he felt one long finger slide all the way back into his now lubricated ass, stroking inside in a way that made his head drop lower in the water. Sound was swallowed as it closed over his ears, framing his face. One of the women fisted her fingers in his hair beneath the waterline, keeping him aware of how easily they could pull him under. Their cruel laughter and comments became gurgles of sound in an echoing chamber where reality and imagination were disturbingly intertwined.

It was harrowing how quickly that straight-edged razor was taking the hair off his privates. Olivia worked the blade with admirably deft skill over him, scraping him clean. When the women's hands moved back over him a few moments later, the hair on his arms, chest, stomach and legs gave way at their touch. The gel was some type of depilatory and cleanser, making him smooth and hairless all over, and explained Mischa's intimate exploration of the area between his buttocks. He had to be as smooth as the proverbial baby's bottom, for Mischa was as thorough as a prison guard doing a drug check. From her smile and the fact he was certain his cock was going to explode, he had no doubt she was enjoying her work.

A guttural sound between pain and pleasure tore out of his throat when Olivia's fingers circled him. She wrapped the straps of the cock harness back around him, increasing the intensity of the near-climactic state he was in. Buckling it over the bare tender skin, she pinched him enough to rein back the response he was sure he couldn't hold back another moment. When the women brought him to his feet, he despised the fact that he was forced to lean as the blood pounded out of his head. Worry and lust made him even more unsteady.

How was he supposed to get a handle on any of this, let alone the upper hand? Mouth stretched by the gag, arms wrenched back to display his chest and hold his muscles taut. Dona's collar on him. He was hard as a rock, his body screaming for release, but thankfully the harness would keep him from losing control. He was terrified to realize he felt like a true slave. Completely out of control, dependent on the whim and Will of his Mistress. A state he'd rarely if ever truly allowed a Mistress to achieve with him.

There would be breathing time later. Wouldn't there? Time to get his ducks in a row. Let them prepare him for her pleasure now. He made himself stand rigid, his jaw clenched as Olivia brought that blade into play on his face. When she made him lift his chin, he could not help but glance toward the banks, seeking Dona. She sat now, her hands clasped around her knees while she watched. Carefully scrutinizing everything being done to him.

Fiona looked toward the shore. "What about his head? Take the hair or wash it?" She had the gel bottle in one hand and another crystal bottle in the other, perhaps shampoo.

Mistresses loved his hair, the thick ash blond strands that they could coil around their fingers, play with on his nape. He'd never let it grow this long, but these last few months he hadn't been interested in letting the prison butchers who called themselves barbers touch it. He'd been looking forward to walking into a men's salon, having it artfully styled the way he always liked it. Short, layered on top, streaked with some dark brown and cut close at his nape, an expensive *GQ*-looking style.

Such a style was part of the whole package that attracted the attention of well-to-do Mistresses who liked a man who knew how to put himself together well. Who would look good on their arm inside a club.

The idea of having another weapon removed from his arsenal panicked him. His ability to assert rights he might not have anymore had been taken from him with that gag. He couldn't employ his charm to coax and cajole. Hell, Dona hadn't even given him a safe word, but he had the distinct feeling they were in a territory far beyond safe words. He was a dumb bastard who had allowed five years of self-denied lust, his weak need to play at being a submissive and the fact he somewhat remembered this bitch to cloud his judgment. He'd been so stupid, giving in to something he felt when he looked at her, some freaky emotional reaction. A reaction that, damn him three times over for an idiot, he still felt every time he looked at her.

Like now, his panicked eyes locking with hers for some type of approbation as she sat on that bank. Her expression said it clearly. He was hers to do with as she wished and it just made his cock get even harder.

Maybe this was some weird hallucination. While his mind howled at the idea he might still be in the prison, undergoing some bad trip on something some bastard had slipped in his slop that was called lunch, no woman had ever had this kind of hold on him.

Pulling away from Olivia, he tried to get away from all of them. He tripped, tumbled under the water. The weeds reached for him, twining around him from ankle to thigh. As he twisted in mindless terror, he sunk further. Tendrils soft as a woman's hair circled his throat under the collar, holding him down below life, air. He struggled, his lungs bursting.

A shadow brushed against him. Feeling a clasp on his arm, he turned his face in that direction, seeking help. Instead, he saw a broad face, the lips pulled back in what would appear to most to be a maternal, kindly look. Her gray and brown hair waved around her face.

*Would you like some candy, sweetie? They're going to let you come home with me. Poor little lost soul…such a pretty child…*

No… He screamed uselessly against the gag as the face got closer, the lips. He was dying and this was what was waiting for him. A cosmic psychotic joke, for it was what he'd spent a lifetime outwitting, escaping… Other shadows moved in and his subconscious knew them all, knew enough about them to make him fight like a berserker against what could not be fought against.

The bindings released. He was rising, hands drawing him up. When his head broke the water's surface, since his arms were still bound behind his back by the manacles, he fought desperately to find and keep his balance, anything to stay up above the waterline, away from what lay below it.

Dona was here. In front of him, with her hands on either side of his neck. They were alone together in the water. The other women sat on the bank, completely dry as if he'd been below the surface for an hour. He blinked through liquid, his gaze coming back to cling to her face. When she removed his gag and stroked his lips, he found himself sucking the water off her fingertips fervently, as if she'd saved him from those awful shadows. Her eyes held mysteries he could not fathom, but she was touching him. All he could figure out in his disoriented state was that his sanity at the moment depended on her not going away.

"What the hell are you doing to me?" He said it hoarsely, resting his head against hers, pressing his cheek against the soft raven strands of her hair. It was so long the ends floated in the water around her hips. Looking down in this position, he saw she wore a black swimsuit now, so sheer that her curves would be starkly defined by the shadowing. Lifting his head to confirm it, he saw her luscious breasts were just above the waterline, the dark circle of her nipples visible behind the transparent netting. Pointed and sharp, as they would be if she were cold. Or aroused.

He pushed his cock against her belly, bending his knees to find the seam of her thighs. Fuck finesse or charm. He'd reverted to pure male animal, needing to reassert who he was. No better way to do that than fucking the woman he wanted.

A sharp yank on his cock snapped his legs back straight like the stock of a rifle. He stifled a yelp, barely. The tether was reattached and back in her hand, wrapped around her wet knuckles.

"Behave, or I'll put you under again." She spoke reprovingly, but when she reached up and brushed her fingertips against his ear she had a gentle touch, mixing up that hard-as-nails way of yanking him in line with a sister-of-mercy touch. She grazed his skull. His bare skull.

"Oh, Jesus." He closed his eyes, shuddering. "Dona. Why..."

"Because you don't need defenses against me, Nathan. Because you'll only make things much worse if you use them."

As she continued to caress his bare pate, he felt...vulnerable. He hadn't expected to feel that way from something as simple as having his head shaved. Each stimulus she inflicted upon him elicited sensations new to him. He was having a hard time sorting it all out. Particularly when he kept losing his anchor on time and reality.

"When..."

"You blacked out a bit. Things will get disorienting here. You need to accept that. Accept my dominance over you and play no games." Her hand went below the water, her fingers rippling along his cock, wrapping around him.

"Dona—"

"I'm going to make you suffer." Her eyes held him, stilled the words in his throat. "You have no choice in that. I'll make it so much worse if you try to fuck with my head. Now..." She let him go and allowed the tether to drop so he felt the weight of it pull against his cock as the chain obeyed gravity and fell toward the bottom. Her bare foot touched his, caressing his toes a moment before she stepped on the top of them. Sliding her arm around his waist, she gripped his forearm, bound against his back, and used it as an anchor to lift herself up. Her breasts pressed against his chest and he had to look at them, draw his breath in and hold it as her hard nipples made contact with his chest. He could feel her thigh against his leg, her hip brushing his eager cock.

"Bring your head down to your Mistress."

He did. As she brushed her lips against his temple, Nathan felt a hard jolt of desire rock through him. She moved to his skull, nibbled. The unfamiliar sensitivity made him thankful for the cock harness. Otherwise he might have come from the brush of her tongue and teeth on that naked flesh. She spoke against his skin, her lips slippery and wet from the water on his skull.

"You're clean enough to come eat my pussy. Follow me."

# Chapter Four

## ∽

She held the leash. Though he tried to stride with some type of dignity, the cock harness dug painfully into him as he stumbled out of the water after her, hands still folded up and bound behind his back. Naked, all his hair removed, reduced to nothing of his identity but being her slave. She moved with the same fluid grace through the water as she had moved over the grass earlier in her high heels, while he had to keep his head bowed to keep his balance. It underscored the picture he imagined he made, humbled in a way he'd never permitted any Mistress to do to him before, but then there'd been no permission involved in this. Except the moment he chose to step into the car.

The back of her swimsuit was as transparent as the front, so as Dona walked ahead of him he saw the cleft between her round buttocks. His Mistress had a generous ass to go with that full bosom, a perfect little hourglass that was spinning him until he was dizzy.

A blanket had been laid on the grass beneath one of the palms. Fiona stood by it. On first glance, Nathan thought she was rubbing suntan lotion on her tawny skin, but then she turned toward them. She was wearing a strap-on, greasing up a dildo of harrowing size fitted into it. The leopard was stretched out nearby, his tail flicking. The narrowed amber eyes watched the bob of the phallus as if he thought it was a toy. It made him uncomfortably aware of his own member, erect and bobbing quite liberally in its harness, enough to attract a cat's attention.

"Mistress." He knew better than to lock his stance now, but he couldn't help dragging his feet at the sight of that mammoth toy. "What—"

"Jonathan, do you wish to be gagged again?"

His jaw flexed. He managed to flick a sullen glance away from the phallus to her face when she stopped at the blanket and turned to face him. "I could hardly serve you properly that way, Mistress."

"No. But I could serve myself while Fiona fucks your ass and you have to watch. Would you rather your mouth have only that ball gag in it?"

"No, Mistress."

"Then you'll do my bidding and not speak unless I ask you a question. While you're on your hands and knees eating me out, your ass will be high in the air and Fiona will be fucking it for my pleasure. It will hurt, so you won't forget yourself and come. You're not going to get to come until I say so, until it's the only thing you can think about, until you believe it's the only thing you've ever wanted. Tell me you understand."

Holding her gaze a moment more than was proper, he spoke softly. "The only thing I want in life is to serve my Mistress. To feel her pussy climaxing around my tongue."

She chuckled scornfully. "That was a well-used line if ever I've heard one. You need some new material."

"Or a permanent gag," Fiona put in.

"As he said, his mouth wouldn't do me much good then, would it?" Dona teased as if they were two schoolgirls, instead of two women planning to split him in two with that huge dildo.

"Come here." She wrapped her hand in Fiona's long hair, grasped her fingers with her other hand and brought the woman closer. Dona rubbed her face along the woman's dusky cheek, freeing one hand to pass her fingers over Fiona's lips. "Show this slave I'm more impressed with silence."

Fiona smiled, leaned in and took Dona's lips in a kiss. Tracing his Mistress's mouth with her tongue, the leopard-skinned woman put her hands to Dona's waist, drew her closer. With eager passion, but also need, affection. There was an emotional exchange occurring as well as physical, telling him Dona had dominated this woman before. These women apparently served her in more ways than one.

Like most men, his cock leaped at the sight of two women touching each other. However, as he watched Fiona's hand caress Dona's lower back, the swell of her hips, slide back up to the side of her breast and her neck to cup her jaw so she could deepen her kiss, something else rose in him. Anger. Jealousy. He wanted Fiona's hands off Dona. Dona was *his* Mistress.

When her tongue tangled with Dona's, she made a sound of pleasure like a growl. Fiona moved closer, bumping the strap-on between Dona's thighs, hinting at what else she could do for her.

"Stop it. *Stop it.*" He surged forward, knocked Fiona away with his shoulder. She stumbled back, her eyes wide, telling him he'd finally been able to do something they didn't expect. His satisfaction with that was short-lived, though, for he'd forgotten about her damn cat.

The leopard snarled and swiped him. Nathan spun away, but not fast enough. The claws caught his upper thigh, raking four stripes through the skin as if it were tissue paper.

*Son of a bitch.* He dropped to one knee, the only thing he could think of to protect his groin. A fetal ball would have been more advisable for that, but he wasn't going to play submissive to an animal. As the cat laid his ears back, Nathan bared his teeth. Snarled. Prepared to body ram the creature if he leaped.

Dona emitted a sharp command and the cat backed off, growling. Fiona put a hand on the spotted ruff, drawing her pet away, both sets of catlike eyes reflecting surprise. Then his Mistress caught his cock tether and yanked him to his feet, a pain he felt all the way to the root that distracted him from the throbbing in his leg.

"Jesus—"

"What the hell do you think you're doing?"

He lunged toward her, anticipating her second pull. His heart was hammering hard against his chest, making words impossible. There was no reason not to take advantage of the moment, though. He placed his mouth over her angry one, fell into her.

Oh, God. Wet heat. Scent. Something so perfect he couldn't describe it. He bit at her lips, needing to taste with more than just his tongue. He wanted to touch her so much he wished he was Samson who could break free of his bonds to draw her close. Touch her the way Fiona had. No, better than Fiona had. Draw her close, hold her completely against him, wrap his arms all the way around and feel her from neck to thigh, knowing she was all his. His Mistress.

They'd dismissed him as if he were simply a misbehaving child. Even with his thigh smarting and knowing how close he'd just come to being disemboweled, he wouldn't be dismissed. Not by her.

Half a heartbeat of bliss and she shoved him away. Wiping her mouth with the back of her hand, she spat on the ground, making him flinch at the cruelty of the gesture.

"You've lost your polish, Jonathan. You're disobedient, rebellious. A pain in the ass. Not the perfect sub I remember hearing so much about."

"No, Mistress." He knew all the moves, all the right things to say, but for some reason he couldn't summon them. As he dropped to one knee before her, he prayed she'd have pity and give him some slack on that tether. She did, sparingly. He felt the strain as she kept his cock stretched, making him feel the pinch on his testicles. "I just don't want anyone else touching you. I'm sorry. I guess I've become...messed up in prison. You tend... You have to fight to keep what's yours. There isn't any sharing."

It was as good an explanation as any, because he'd be damned if he could explain it himself. He bowed his head, staring at her bare feet, the dark wine-colored polish on her pretty toes.

After a long, tense moment, those toes moved away. When Nathan raised his head, she was settling herself nearby on several pillows her ladies arranged for her, as if attending an empress before she was serviced by her favored pet.

Fiona squatted before him, that massive strap-on brushing his quivering leg. She'd apparently recovered her aplomb, for with an impatient nudge of her knuckles against his inner thigh, she indicated she wanted both his knees on the ground and spread apart. When he reluctantly complied, she slapped a wet cloth on his thigh. The smell and the fiery burning told him it was soaked with alcohol.

He bit the inside of his cheek to stay still and quiet and held her gaze with one as unflinching as her own. Once the dampness had molded the compress to his thigh, she hooked another tether to the cock harness, to the ring that was positioned beneath his scrotum. The pressure of her knuckles on the base of his cock made him leak another drop. Swiping her finger over it, she took it to the strap-on and rubbed it over the head, giving him a taunting look. When he curled his lip at her, she chuckled, gave him a hard slap along his dick that made him grit his teeth. Rising, she pulled off the compress and went behind him to thread the leash up between his buttocks and through the space between his folded and bound forearms. Her cold fingers wrapped around his throat as she held him steady to run the strap through several of the rings running along the back of the collar.

Now he had a tether running from genitals to throat, a rein held snug on his back by his own manacled arms and Fiona's ruthless hold, while Dona still held the tether attached to the harness around the base of his cock.

As Dona began to reel in that tether, he had to walk awkwardly on his knees to her. Like a wild animal being led from a cage, one handler holding tension from behind while one maintained it forward. Dona spread her legs, showing him her pussy through the sheer fabric. Her fingers lay on her thigh, a whisper away from caressing herself.

The sunlight glistened off the silken netting, denying him a fully unimpeded view. He had the unexpected thought he would walk on his knees forever to reach such an offering. He balked, despite his body's scream of protest. Why was she affecting him this way? She'd come to get him at the prison because she wanted him. She'd said so. Why would that unbalance him so much? Other women had wanted him.

Other women had wanted Jonathan Powell. She had come for Nathan.

Fiona shoved him forward abruptly. Before he could land face first on the blanket, he was brought up short by her firm grip on the collar, her nails scratching his skin. Her brace against the tether put an aching tension from cock to arms to throat. The collar hobbled his air flow enough she could control him, but he hovered right over Dona's cunt, his ass in the air as she'd described. In his current position, he could only stare at those pink folds of skin, the tender lips compressed behind the mesh. As he breathed shallowly, he could smell her arousal. That aroma matched the intent look of her eye, her parted wet mouth. Those beautiful breasts rose like gentle hills above the satin terrain of her abdomen. He could see the jutting nipples as she reclined. Straining forward like an eager dog in truth, he felt the muscles in his shoulders bunch with the effort.

He cursed as a crop snapped sharply down on his flank. Mariah stood off to the side with it, tossing her red hair over her pale shoulder.

"Behave, slave, or you'll eat nothing but dirt."

When he snarled, they laughed at him, but he noted with satisfaction that Fiona decided to change her position. The woman's tawny legs came down on either side of his hips, her thighs pressing against him to give her better leverage to hold him back. The weight of the dildo against his spine drove away the moment of triumph, reminding him that she was about to put that thing in him. What would they do if he bucked her off and plunged his mouth into that juicy cunt taunting his eyes, his nose? It took effort to discard the appealing notion. He had to convince Dona he could be an obedient sub. That was the way he played the game. When he stuck to that strategy, he always won.

That conviction had always been strong in his mind, like the first mark of a lead pencil on the page of a test. As he spent time with each Mistress, the page became filled with words, the right answers that would bring the right results. Now the thought bit at his gut, like the dull ache of an ulcer. The game had a structure, a rating, a result. But ultimately, what did it mean?

Five years in prison. Five years of lying in the darkness, being chased by shadows. The same shadows that had moved under the water when they bathed him. Shadows that flitted through Dona's eyes now as he looked at her.

What if he didn't want it to be about the game? Maybe he just didn't want to disappoint her.

*Jesus Christ, Powell. Does she already own you?*

Fuck the game. He'd knock Fiona back on her skinny ass and prove to Dona he wasn't to be fucked with, her and her shadows. He wanted it to be between the two of them. He wanted to see if his Mistress could take him, bring him to heel when she went toe-to-toe with the savage animal that he truly was. No pretenses.

The desire to completely let go rolled over him with the force of murderous rage. Muscles tensed in his shoulders, his thighs bunching to propel himself off the ground.

Dona sat up abruptly, laid her hand on his jaw.

"Sssh, my pet. Calm. You can do this. I need your mouth. I need you."

He met her gaze, that soft brown deer color, and he couldn't follow through on it. The bite of the passion was there, but with that one softly spoken command, she held him in place. While he couldn't make his muscles move, he was afraid it wasn't the weird magic of this place. In his chest was a burning that said he *wanted* to obey, to please her.

His moment of opportunity had slipped from his fingers with the simple touch of her hand. As Dona lay back, her hand falling away from him, Mischa positioned his ass even higher up in the air, the way they apparently wanted it for Fiona's penetration. Olivia and Fiona roughly jerked his knees out even wider, making him even more dependent on Fiona's pressure on the leash to keep his balance. He coughed at the increased pressure on his throat, which kept him occupied with breathing. When he focused on that waiting pussy, his tongue swiped his own lips.

"First the pain. To earn my pleasure." Dona's voice, touching his ears like her fingertips.

Mariah knelt on one side of him, Olivia the other. Gripping his buttocks, they spread him open as Fiona backed up, the dildo making an oily path up his spine. He tried not to tense as she guided herself in, moving the strap of the leash out of her way between his buttocks. He thanked whatever deities might be responsible for her liberal lubrication, but it was a large cock and he was far from relaxed. Being well aware she couldn't care less about being gentle made his tension worse.

The burning started, making him need more oxygen than he was getting. He managed the pain, his breath rasping in and out, in and out. Christ, it was excruciating. He kept his eyes on the goal, the only thing that mattered. He'd give Dona pleasure for the pain, replace her cool reserve with gasping, wide-eyed arousal. He could smell how wet she was without that damned latex in the way. He sensed her anticipation and it fired his own blood to raging.

But, Jesus, the cat woman was going to kill him first, split him in two. Despite himself, a grunt of distress came from his lips as she slid forward another inch, the tight inner muscles giving way reluctantly. His eyes were tearing from the agony as she sank deep. It was a good thing he'd always been a hard-core sub, able to take extremes of pain and still come at his Mistress's command, but this was pressing the boundaries of even his high limits.

"It's in." Her fingernails whispered down his back. Her thighs pressed flat against him. He'd never felt so invaded, his cock turgid in the harness and his ass impaled on the rigid phallus.

Dona's voice was sex wrapped in silk. "It stays in until you make me come."

The lust surged through his blood, the fire of one dragon meeting the flame of another, red pain meeting red passion so together they became inseparable.

Fiona's hold on the collar eased enough so his lips could reach Dona. Just barely, so he had to strain and work all the harder for it. He wanted to descend on her like a rutting stag, but something checked that impulse. Maybe it was the discipline of a lifetime he'd used to play upon a woman's desires. Or maybe it was his own desire to see how much pleasure he could give her. He didn't really give a damn about the whys at the moment.

Taking his head down a millimeter at a time, he let his breath caress her first, make her feel the promise of moisture in it. He saw her draw in a breath, hold it, her teeth biting her bottom lip. God if that sexy gesture didn't make his cock pulse dangerously even in the restrictive harness. When his lips finally pressed against the mesh, he felt the give of her cunt lips beneath his mouth, the most intimate of kisses. He couldn't help closing his eyes, drawing her aroma in through his nose. Opening his mouth wide now, he closed over her entirely and tickled her with the tip of his tongue through the netting, a tiny caress between those lips. A promise that he would thrust his tongue thick and deep into her if she'd just give him the chance.

Fiona started to thrust, which would have pushed him more aggressively against Dona's pussy if he hadn't held himself back. He didn't want to go there yet. He wanted Dona to reach for him, show him he was making an impact. Though the parted lips, the elevated breathing and the arch of her back that tilted up those incredible tits were signs, he wanted more. He fought the pain for it.

"Ah, he's a stubborn one, Dona." Fiona breathed it, working in him, her nails pinching into the upper part of his buttocks while Mariah and Olivia continued to grip either side, keeping him spread, kneading him, crooning over what a fine ass he had.

Dona seized him, fingers grasping his bare skull. She pistoned her hips, burying his face in her pussy.

It was as effective as a barked order. His Mistress wanted his passion, the beast in him. The erratic clutch of her hands, the way she bared her throat with rigid intensity told him so.

He caught the mesh in his teeth, tore it away and thrust his tongue fully into her before there was time for her or Fiona to do anything to stop him.

She gasped, the sound music to his ears. Her grip tightened on his head, holding him as he fucked her with his tongue, sucked on her clit appreciatively and delved deeper into her cunt. The burning pain was so potent now he was shaking with it, his body covered with sweat, the nausea in his gut matching the guttural sounds of stress coming from his throat, sounds of raw need. Even as the lust drove him, he knew he couldn't take much more of the torture without screaming for mercy.

Fiona unbuckled the strap-on and expertly wove its straps around his waist, hips and buttocks, creating a net of restraints to hold it in him without the pressure of her body. When she cinched in the final crosstie at the small of his back, it drove the dildo in deeper. He cried out. In mindless reaction to the terrible pain and lust intertwined, he bit Dona. Sinking his teeth into either side of her outer labia, he held on and kept his tongue deep inside her.

He should have been kicked away. Instead, his eyes flicked up wild and frenzied to see her lips draw back from her teeth in a primitive snarl. Her nails dug into his newly shaved scalp, drew blood of her own as she began to climax. With his breath hot on her pussy, his lips pressed to her, he felt her convulse under him. It made him feel something he couldn't give a name. Didn't want to. Through the clench of his teeth he tasted her. Sweet as Kahlua. Smooth, the bitter overlaid by the sweet.

She bucked against him, making harsh sounds of release, her lips parted. He watched her, caught between the lust tearing up his insides and a still wonder at the way she looked. Her breasts, moving generously with her body's undulations. The curve of her throat, the way her cheeks and upper body flushed from the climax. So overwhelming to his senses even their torment couldn't keep him from being riveted by it.

Only when she began to drift down did the grip of his jaws ease, his tongue lapping, mouth savoring that faint flavor, wondering at its mixture with her musky taste. His ass quivered, his inner muscles screaming even as they milked that dildo involuntarily, seeking a release.

Her legs now lay on his shoulders, one thigh trembling against his jaw so that it was the most natural thing in the world to turn his head, press a hard kiss to the skin, rub against her in jerky, aroused movements.

Her eyes opened and focused on him, watched him as he continued to kiss her there. Forcing himself to turn the volume down, he made the kisses more tender. His cock throbbed and his ass burned so badly his eyes were running with moisture that met his lips where they touched her skin. It was okay. He knew how to handle pain. Could push it back to give her pleasure.

She probably didn't know he knew about this part. That he didn't understand the intense, indescribable feeling a male slave derived from serving his Mistress. There had been moments like this, when he'd gotten immersed in giving his Mistress pleasure. A part of him had known it contributed to the game he was playing with her head. Another part of him got lost in the euphoria of it, seeing his Mistress arch into climax and knowing he'd been responsible for that ecstasy.

Her lips parted, tongue touching them as if she was wetting them to speak from a dry throat. But before she could, Fiona yanked at his collar, dragging him back from the touch of Dona's body.

*No, dammit.* Throwing his weight forward, he toppled the feline woman against his back and earned an agonizing rocket of pain as she knocked into the strap-on.

He'd been at the high end of the scale with that dildo up his ass. This was like having a hot poker added to the mix. The agony drove away rational thought and left only a killing rage. He turned on Fiona. The abrupt movement yanked the tether from her grip, but without any way to balance himself he tumbled over, slamming to the ground onto one shoulder. Thank God Dona had dropped her tether at some point during his pleasuring of her, or his dick would have been yanked off.

As his knees drew up in a fetal position, Nathan wished he wasn't in such horrid pain so that he could get to Fiona and snap her damn neck. The leopard arched just behind her legs, fuzzed up, teeth bared in a menacing hiss.

*That's right. You hide back there, Fluffy. You know I'll whip your spotted ass. Jesus, I'm dying here.*

Then Dona was there, her hand on his brow soothing him, even as he rocked with the pain. One hand brushed his belly and loosened the straps while her other hand caressed his buttock. A moment later she gripped the torture device and eased it out of him. His tender tissues wept in relief so that he couldn't stop himself from groaning.

He'd had a lot of competent Mistresses. Hell, the best. That's why he went after them in the first place. Mistresses who liked to play on the far edge loved him because he was able to keep his cock hard under all forms of duress. However, Dona took the scale of intense arousal and pain to a whole new level. The best opponent he'd ever had and he hadn't even chosen her.

His cock still throbbed with frustration, her scent heavy under his nose, on his lips. Just the press of her body behind him made his lust spike higher, even though he might be bleeding to death from his ass. Struggling to his back despite the discomfort of rolling onto his bound arms, he stared up at her. He was surrounded by some of the finest pussy he'd ever seen, but it was hers specifically he wanted to look at, to touch. He wanted to hear her command him to fuck her. He would do it well, make her want to take him home, keep him at her bidding until…

Until he was done with her. Until he broke her. Because he always had a finish line.

She tilted her head, her fingers stroking over his chest, pinching his nipples. "You misbehaved. You're required to take any level of pain from me without complaint, with devotion and beg for more. That's what I demand from my slave. Stretch out your legs and spread them for me."

He did. As he lifted his head, this time he was able to see the ground slither, undulate. Before he could jerk away, ropes of green grass ran around his ankles and thighs, anchored him to the ground. The same now came across his forehead and chest, yanking his head back down, holding him fast, immobile. The strain on his shoulders from his folded arms increased exponentially. The confidence he'd momentarily felt at knowing he'd brought her pleasure evaporated.

"What is this place?" He couldn't keep the panic out of his voice. The women were descending on him again. They marched forward with the deliberate forward progress of zombie armies in B-movies. Indifferent to the cries of their victims and driven only by hunger. Mariah now carried a black satchel. As she knelt by him and opened it for Dona's inspection, he saw it had a variety of needles and clamps in it.

Fiona stepped to Dona's side, drawing her attention away from him.

"He wants to see you," she murmured. "Right away."

"Then I'll go to Him," his Mistress responded.

"Dona, what are you... What are they... Please..." He was too desperate to articulate.

Rising, she put her foot on his chest. In a blink, instead of the swimsuit she was back in her first outfit, the stiletto heel grinding into his chest, those full breasts once again high and proud. "Do you know what to do with a Mistress's foot, Nathan?"

He stared up at her. As if in a dream, he kissed the sole of the boot she pressed to his lips so he tasted the dirt and grass she'd walked through. "This isn't real," he said when she lifted her foot away. He tasted the grit in his teeth.

"It's very real. It's also illusion. That's what makes it possible for the pain to go on and on."

His eyes snapped over to Olivia as she lifted her hand, displaying four D-rings and a handful of wide barbells. Dona nodded. "Those will do."

"Will do what? What are you doing?" Though he was very afraid he knew what. He was beginning to have a feeling he hadn't had in a long time, a feeling he'd never wanted to have again. Plotting for control of the situation would not only be foolish, but futile. Somehow Dona seemed to know his darkest areas, where desire and terror were violent bed partners.

"I have to go away for a while, as Fiona said."

"Who is 'him'?" It was ridiculous that he could feel jealousy in the midst of all of this, but there it was.

"One who can't be refused. Just like me." Bending, she cupped the side of his face in a surprisingly gentle hand. He wanted to weep and suckle that fluttering pulse at once. He tried the latter, but she was out of reach and he was too restrained, which made him want to rage even harder against his bonds, the situation.

This should have seemed like his time with his previous sociopath of a Mistress, but it didn't. She hadn't made him jealous while threatening him with sharp implements. She hadn't left him wanting more, even with his ass smarting so badly he wouldn't have easy bodily functions for a week. She hadn't made him tremble with just a touch.

"You'll refuse me nothing, will you?"

He found himself nodding even as he wondered what spell she'd cast on him. "Just don't go to him."

"Your slave is possessive, Dona," Olivia murmured. Nathan didn't hear any mockery in her tone or expression. If anything, she looked as if his uncensored declaration had startled her.

"Nathan will learn my Will is his only possession." Dona straightened, giving him a leisurely perusal. Under her intent regard, Mariah removed the cock harness and caressed his broad head, making his hips jerk because he was so aroused.

"While I'm gone," Dona said almost absently, watching Mariah fondle him, "Fiona will pierce your nipples and your cock. You'll have a ring inserted at the crown so I can attach a leash to you more easily. She'll also insert one in your scrotum for when I wish to collar your balls with weights and stretch them." When Mariah pushed his organ flat against his belly, letting Dona see the underside, she sharpened her gaze on him there, creating a cold ball of fear in his vitals. "Four barbells will be inserted along the bottom length of your cock, a ladder. I want to climb it with my fingers, weave all sorts of chains and beads into it to decorate you as I wish."

His airway squeezed down to the size of a straw, the terror of the picture putting him on the edge of hyperventilating. Underscoring her threat, the women were removing the clamps and needles from the satchel. "I..." He swallowed on a dry throat. "I want to be able to serve you as you wish, Mistress. You know the piercing will take a lot of healing time."

Those red wet lips lifted in a grim smile. "Pain is an illusion here. It will go on as long and intensely as I wish you to experience it. So until I get back you'll be in agony. You'll feel the throbbing pain of the piercings in their newness. It's a considerable amount of pain." Her eyes flashed in anticipation of it. At the sign of her arousal in contemplating it, damn if his cock didn't bob up further.

"Ah, Nathan. You're a pleasure. It makes me even wetter, the way you respond to my desire. When I come back, if you've pleased me, I'll heal you with a kiss on each area. You'll be able to serve me any way I wish. The stimulation of the nerve endings after the piercing is healed is...a unique feeling." Her gaze came back to his, full of sensual promise. Gooseflesh rose along his body at the sight of it. "You might just stay erect for me most of the time. Of course, you seem to stay that way for me now. It's very impressive."

"Come down here and let me impress you more." His voice was desperate, even to his own ears.

She tsked at him. "With your size, I like keeping you fully erect. It will keep you dizzy and off balance. That's a good thing for you."

"Dona—" He clenched his fists in his restraints as she turned away. As Fiona raised the first needle and Olivia put the clamp on his left nipple, lifting it, he cried out, unable to bear it anymore. "*Tell me what the fuck this place is.*"

She glanced over her shoulder. He tried to cling to her expression and not look at what was about to happen to him. The binding on his forehead loosened. Seizing his collar, Mariah cupped the back of his head, forcing it down so he had to watch the needle come toward his nipple. He strained against her grip, trying to get one more glimpse of his Mistress.

"You know where we are, Jonathan." Dona raised her arms and spun, gesturing to the palm trees, lush grass and mirror-like lagoon, the gently shining sun. "This is Hell."

As she stepped through a portal that opened like a shimmering mirage between two palm trees, he began to scream.

# Chapter Five

§Ɔ

Lucifer summoned her to one of His more pleasant illusion chambers. This one was like a gentleman's study in a Victorian novel. Except an inordinately large fire roared in the grate and the pictures on the walls tended to shift in macabre images. The gargoyle statues positioned around the room might be alive or inanimate from moment to moment.

He sat in a deep wing-backed chair. Approaching at His gesture, she dropped to her knees. Bowing her head, Dona felt that inexplicable desire she always felt in His presence, to just put her head in His lap and be comforted where no comfort could be had.

"Now you're submissive and obedient." He snorted. The wave of heat from the gesture brought sulfur to her nostrils. "Moments ago you were defiant as a child. 'This *is* my home', indeed."

"This is my home, my Lord. Where I want to be."

"This is not where you want to be. This is where you hide."

"Do I not serve you well here?"

When she felt His regard over His cup of wine, she raised her gaze. He was everything the books said. The fallen angel, too beautiful to be real, but also not exactly what they thought He was. He had many names, none of which was completely accurate or defined him. He was as much Hades to the Greeks as He was Satan to the Christians or the Horned God to the pagans. He could be the shadow in the night or the mightiest of the angels serving a terrible, fearful purpose. The purpose that provided a fallen soul a new beginning when it was needed. Or the bridge to continue the journey to enlightenment.

She didn't mind the smell of sulfur anymore, any more than she minded the smell of death, rotting flesh, or sounds of pain. Those things were pure in their intent here. While she did not presume to know a tenth of the mysteries that governed the Being before her, she knew He never lied to her. Even when she wanted Him to do so.

"You serve me well here." He inclined His head. "You've taken at least a thousand souls through Redemption, delivered them to the Hall of Souls for their return to Purgatory. Perhaps somehow that's made you believe you belong here. I've watched you be stimulated by your skill with them, the way an artist is enthralled by how her hand moves a paintbrush on blank canvas. Out of all those thousand souls, you've not once been stimulated by the creation itself. Until now."

Unbidden, she saw Nathan in her mind. The smooth firmness of his lips, his broad palms. It was not difficult to imagine his long fingers stroking her skin. Penetrating her body as he watched her with eyes that were so blue the lagoon and the sky couldn't match their intensity. His body was sleek lines of muscle, tough and hard where she was soft. Where she ached for hardness.

When Nathan had shoved Fiona from her, she'd been glad he'd fallen to his knees and bowed his head. He was far too intuitive and it wouldn't have taken much intuition to see the tremor in her hand, the pulse pounding high in her throat. She hadn't seen his possessive reaction coming. It had been a long time since anything had surprised her. That brief brush of his firm lips against hers had been like the barest hint of a rich chocolate, taken away before it could be fully sampled. His body so close, the heat of that hard muscular body, the aroused cock close enough to brush her skin…

Great Lucifer, the way he'd crouched, thighs taut and ready, eyes focused and dangerous, his lip curled back to snarl at the leopard.

At that moment, she realized she'd assumed he was a coward, like so many others in his life had. There apparently was an important difference between being opportunistic and craven. The man had courage. Where there was courage, there could be integrity.

She told herself that it was good she'd broken the kiss before things had gotten out of hand. Even though her body wasn't so sure of that, even now.

If it was just physical, she would welcome the images. Like a candy bar she could consume, enjoy and discard the wrapper. But those firm lips could smile. Those blue eyes could be angry, tender, puzzled, intrigued. Thousands of expressions and she wanted to see every one of them. Every pain he'd suffered bludgeoned her heart. Every crime he'd committed tore at her soul. If he genuinely smiled, teased her without malice, she knew she'd do anything to rescue him from himself.

For a moment she hated the Being in front of her, though she knew she might as well hate herself, since all He was showing her was what was in her own heart. She bowed her forehead to the ground, found some reassurance in the position, almost a fetal crouch of self-comfort. "I don't want it to be true, my Lord," she whispered. "I don't want a soul mate."

The fire crackled. His foot was close. When she pressed her cheek to the heated stone next to it, she studied the illusion of toenails, bone. If she closed her hand on the flesh, it would feel solid, real, even though it was just a form Lucifer assumed to give her a point of reference. Nathan was like that. Everything he appeared to be wasn't real. It was her job to tear away an illusion that he'd adhered to himself like skin, rip it all away, leave the raw nerves exposed and let the screams of agony from his soul guide him back to the man he was supposed to be.

"If I could have spared you the pain, I would have, child. You know that."

"I know that. You gave me the choice."

Lucifer had called her to Him much like this, almost a month ago. He'd told her Jonathan Powell would be entering their domain soon.

Over five years ago, she'd assumed a corporeal form to spend time at The Zone, a fetish club on the mortal plane. Her purpose had been to monitor a murderess who would soon enter Lucifer's domain. Hell's version of administrative work. Nathan had been involved with the woman. That relationship had sent him to prison and lead to the fatal knife fight, so close to the end of his five-year sentence. The fight which had brought him to the illusion of a dusty ribbon of asphalt, waiting for his Mistress of Redemption to retrieve him.

During the time she'd been doing the survey work on the S&M Killer, she couldn't stop watching him, being absorbed by everything about him. She didn't want to feel that way, couldn't understand how she knew his real name was Nathan and why she was certain he belonged to her, though they were divided by the plane between life and death.

Lucifer wasn't in the habit of calling her into His presence to notify her personally of arrivals, but His reasons became clear when He gave a name to the connection between her and the mortal who looked like a blond Norse god.

*You feel this way for him because he is your soul mate. You will feel him the moment he enters our world, which is why I am telling you he is coming. He is a difficult case. The best thing for him is Hell. I will let the fires and torments purify his soul, erase all that he is. Then he can begin his life cycles over again from the beginning, as it must be with those who have gotten so lost.*

Her response to that hadn't been a conscious decision. Her heart screaming in protest at the idea, she opened her mouth before she even knew herself what she was going to say.

*I can redeem him. I know I can do it. Let me do my job.*

Dona closed her eyes, remembering the conversation. "I'll do my job," she said.

"That's what concerns me." She felt His heat as He bent over her, His voice a quiet rumble. "Even when you lived as a mortal years ago, you sought this man, though your conscious mind didn't know it. Your fetish clubs considered you somewhat of a dangerous Mistress because you pushed your submissives so hard. You were practicing. Waiting for him. Anticipating his need. The true bad boy, the one so far gone down the dark path you'd have to risk your own soul to bring him back. I shouldn't have been swayed by your desire."

"You knew there was a chance I could do it, my Lord. Else you wouldn't have permitted it."

There was a significant pause. The pressure in the room increased, sending a surge of terror through her. Why had she not guarded her tongue? She was not concerned for herself, but for Nathan. She had to finish. Had to succeed.

"I can't let him go to Hell without trying my best, my Lord. If I let him go to save myself anguish, I've sentenced him without a fair trial."

"Dona, you do not sentence souls. I do. If I send him into Hell, it is because his soul deserves purification—"

"I *am* sentencing him, if I let him go that way. I can't—"

His voice cut across hers. "Whether or not he can be redeemed is irrelevant. You believe he can be because there is no other choice for a soul mate. You have faith in him, even when he is undeserving of it."

"My lord, I have the objectivity to do this. When I saw him at The Zone, when I was there at your bidding, I never touched him. Never approached him."

"I don't know if that makes you the most disciplined minion I have, or the loneliest." Before she could say anything further, He reached down and touched her.

The sulfur, the fire and all the trappings just vanished. It was only her soul, tired and afraid, surrounded by the warmth and power of His essence, the white light of divinity that connected Him to the All moving around her, embracing her, giving her His pity and forgiveness. She felt the irresistible tug of it, the screaming desire it created to go to the Hall of Souls, the privilege she'd earned but could not face. Hell could cleanse a woman's soul, but it couldn't heal the fears of a shattered heart, no matter how many years had passed.

The touch gave her something else she didn't want. It forced her to experience her connection to Nathan in its full power, a link she'd only been able to face in small, controlled pieces on her own. The energy rolled over her and tore her shields away, letting her feel her soul mate's proximity, every touch she'd shared with him, hear every word he'd uttered. It was like having her skin ripped away a strip at a time. In his presence she felt alive, passionate. She wasn't lonely. She hadn't felt that way in so long. Hadn't wanted to feel that way, not even now.

Even Nathan, trapped in the evil he'd allowed to take him over, had felt it. She saw it in his eyes, his confusion warring with the frightened rage that stoked his desire to hurt her if she showed a moment of weakness. She cursed the so-called gift of soul mates that allowed her to see the man behind all of it, the man she loved with everything she was.

She touched the energy, weeping. When it withdrew, it did so slowly, not unkindly, leaving her back in the study with Lucifer.

"Yes, he senses it too. But he does not have what he needs to truly understand why he responds to you this way, why he wants so badly to serve you. It's not your time to be together. He's got much further to go."

"I can help him get on the right path." She tasted her tears on the seam of her lips. "Professional pride, my Lord. I started the task. Please..." She swallowed. "I beg you. Let me finish it."

"I'm afraid it will finish you."

She opened her mouth, but He waved her away. "I gave you my word. Go back and see what you can do with him. Just remember, when you're done, he's gone." His brows drew down. "So are you. It's time for you to return to living. Your debt is paid and your place is no longer here."

"I have a choice—"

"So do I. To fire you." His lips curved without humor. "That leaves you nowhere to go but the Hall of Souls."

Even she knew when not to argue with the Devil, though her heart seethed with frustration. She nodded, rose to her feet and backed out of the chamber, quelling a very childish urge to slam the heavy oak door, illusion though it was.

*Don't even think of it. I already have a headache from you as it is.*

"What will you do? Spank me?" she muttered.

Lucifer sent her spinning out of His plane with a mere flicker of a thought, knowing she'd land hard before the portal to the oasis reality, possibly with palm tree fronds up her defiant backside. The spark of humor that flickered through Him was brief, however. Tossing the goblet into the fire, He curled His lip back in a snarl. "He's dragging her down, as I said he would. We will destroy her with this madness."

The flames shifted and He saw Her face there, the suggestion of the body that She'd chosen for the moment.

"You care about her. But this meeting between them was meant to be. Soul mates cannot deny their bonds here. You said as much to her."

"This man has dedicated his mortal life to destroying the souls of women. You know what could happen to her soul if it is destroyed by her own soul mate. It's not him I worry about. The Cycle will take him where he needs to go."

"You had to do something. Her soul mate, as immature as he yet is, may do what we have been unable to do. Make her believe that she is deserving of love again. Perhaps the two of them together can accomplish what they cannot alone." The fire flared out, surrounding Him. He passed his fingers through it, feeling Her within as well as without. "Love creates miracles, my Lord. That is what we are. Dona is strong, one of the strongest Mistresses of Redemption who has ever served you. Have faith."

"Faith is your department. Justice is mine."

Her soft breath touched Him. "Oh, you are so wrong, dearest. How could I have the faith to come out and shine in the fullness of the moon at night if I did not feel the heat of your rays lingering from the daylight warming me? Your justice is balanced by my mercy, but my mercy comes from the love you give me as a gift. For every half a heart there is another heart. You could have cast him into Hell's fires, but since he is hers, you gave her the choice. You have faith."

"Know me so well, do you?" His brow quirked, a mortal gesture, but one She enjoyed, evidenced by the fact She raised fingers of flame that were cool as water and stroked it, reached in and touched the light energy of Him, twining it with Her own.

"As I know my own heart. We are One, as we have always been."

\* \* \* \* \*

They were done. Mariah sat on the grass several yards from Nathan, combing out her copper red hair and watching the leopard play with the fiery ends. They'd released her slave's head and neck, taken his arms from behind his back and tethered them out to his sides with some slack, but his ankles and thighs remained bound. The D-rings gleamed at his nipples and the head of his cock, making her lust stir despite the emotional upheaval her visit to Lucifer had caused her.

As Dona circled him, she saw the silver of the one in his scrotum. It was just visible under the fold of his cock. They'd cleaned up the blood, but he was pale, bathed in sweat from what she was certain was throbbing, excruciating pain. His jaw was tight, his teeth clamped on a metal bit they'd placed between his teeth and fastened tightly around his head, stretching the corners of his mouth cruelly. Fiona's doing, she was sure. The leopard woman had an appealing vindictive streak.

Squatting, Dona lifted his semi-erect member and examined the ladder of barbells they'd run all the way up from the base to below the flare of the head. They'd hooked a chain to each bar and latched the end to the scrotum ring so as he became fully erect the tension would pull on all the inserted metal bars, increasing the sensation.

She was tempted to stroke him, see if she could do just that. Holding him like this so intimately, feeling him watching her every movement, unable to speak to her, made her want to do even more. Take him somewhere that wasn't about Redemption, Hell or anything other than just exploring this fluttery tug of feeling as he watched her.

What would it be like, to have the leisure to do that? She hadn't thought of the things of the mortal world in some time, not in relation to herself. Now she visualized herself in her living room, the gas logs flickering. Maybe it was a Friday night and they'd planned to go out to a club. She was in a short blue silk dress that fit like a second skin. He wore slacks and a dress shirt that strained over his broad shoulders as he went to his knees before her and tried to tease her into staying home. His lips nibbling up her ankle, his gaze full of nothing but her and hot desire as he tried to coax her into parting her legs. She imagined pushing him back. Perhaps he'd resist her at first, prove to her he was stronger by capturing her and rolling her to the floor, holding her pinned under him as he teased her neck with his mouth, pressed his hardness beneath the slacks between her legs.

Because he knew he was her slave, which had nothing to do with strength, at length he'd obey her and roll to his back. Tremors would run through those fine muscles as she stroked him, made him stay still at her command. Opening his dress shirt, she'd spread it out to look at his fine chest. She'd stand over him, straddling him so he'd get teasing glances of the bare skin in the shadows beneath her short skirt. As she performed a slow, writhing dance over him, one hand playing with the folds of the skirt, inching it up, the other rising to trace the curve of her breast in the plunging neckline, she'd tease him with her words as well.

She'd tell him how she planned to take him to the club, make him sit at a table on the edge of the dance floor while she did a fuck-me-now dance just like this, attracting the attention of other men. She knew her slave, knew how possessive and jealous he could get.

She'd dance out under the flashing strobe lights, watch his eyes get more heated until she could feel the violent need of his passion at a hundred paces, his fury with the men who dared get near his Mistress. Only then would she call him to her so she could do that sensual dance against him, prove that he was the only one she wanted. She'd make him agonizingly hard so all the women would see and be envious if they didn't have such a fine, large cock to call their own.

As she taunted him with the picture in their living room, she'd slowly peel the dress away from her flesh, the firelight dappling her skin. He'd beg her to fuck him then. Knees pressing into the carpet, she'd go down on him, her heart full of the look in his face, her skin shivering under his touch as he disobeyed and reached for her, overwhelmed by the feeling swamping them both...

That was what she would do with Nathan. Jonathan had no place in her fantasy. His alter ego had the upper hand in him right now, his malice and fear infecting his actions the same way they infected his soul.

Evil preyed on fear and insecurity. Used it as the pathway to dig into a soul, corrupt and turn it. Her job was no different from an exorcist's. With surgical precision, she removed the tentacles of evil that grew around the soul and reminded it of its strength and purity. If the evil had already permeated it, then the soul was beyond her help. The scalding fires of Hell were needed to burn it to ashes. Like a phoenix, it would be reborn, with no memory of any lessons learned.

As Lucifer had implied, Nathan was a borderline case. Decay was a spider web throughout his soul, but the mass of it was on the outside, not in the marrow. Hell would be the most efficient solution, no doubt. But because he was connected to her in a way she couldn't deny, she couldn't accept that Hell's fire was his fate. It made her angry, because she knew Lucifer was never wrong.

She'd told herself repeatedly that soul mates were just an instinct, a physical addiction that had forced open her mouth and made her beg to take him on. Eventually, as Lucifer had said, she'd have to release Nathan, whether to Hell or to Purgatory. Really, it was a relief to know she didn't *have* to resist this feeling. She could explore it as much as she wanted without danger to herself, because he was going to be taken from her whether she could bear to let him go or not.

She was so tired. It was an unusual feeling down here where needs of the body could be optional, though lust and sex in this instance had been turned on full force to tap into Nathan's soul where he was most vulnerable. One of her strongest compulsions in her mortal life was her most expertly used tool here, the ability to sexually dominate a man.

He reminded her of the tender side of that compulsion. Things she'd long ago lost faith in, such that Hell had seemed a better place to be than anything the Hall of Souls or reincarnation could offer.

*I'll do the job. Then it will be over. I'll figure out a way to convince Lucifer to let me stay, so I never have to go down that road again.* There were people who thought that refusing to go forward was stagnation. She knew progress was just a mislabeled road sign for "this way to self-annihilation".

"Beautifully done, ladies." Dropping onto her knees next to his head at last, she gazed down into his lovely blue eyes. In them she saw agony, fury, fear...and relief to see her. She could tell that confused the hell out of him. Her heart twisted in her chest with understanding. She wasn't any less confused just because she had the ability to give the connection between them a name.

Reaching around his head, she removed the bit and guided it out of his mouth, touching Nathan's finely shaped lips as she did so. She noted the redness and blue bruising at his nipples, same as at his cock. From the strain in his face, she knew he was still feeling the pain keenly. Yet his hand rose, albeit trembling with that agony. She watched, mesmerized as he almost made it to her face before the restraints on his arms brought him up short. When she leaned forward, closing the distance, he cupped her cheek, his thumb brushing her jaw just below her lips, as if he did not dare to presume so much as to touch her mouth.

"Did he hurt you?" he asked thickly. He'd apparently bitten his tongue, explaining why they'd employed the bit as an afterthought. "It looks...in your eyes. It looks like he did."

She looked for charm or duplicity in his expression. While she didn't see any, she knew he was very clever. Because she saw the soul that was Nathan speaking through him, trying to struggle through the wreckage Jonathan had made of him, she gave him honesty back. "That's what those who love you do. God's no different in that."

His eyes crinkled, his lips drawing back into a grimace, showing her that the corners of his mouth were torn by the bit. His body shuddered with a harsh chuckle. "I always...figured...God ran Hell."

*If he genuinely smiled, teased her without malice, she knew she'd do anything to rescue him from himself.*

Fiona had returned to Dona's side. Dona felt the leopard press against her back. She reached back, found his chin and gave him a passing scratch, though her gaze remained on Nathan.

"He's having an endorphin rush. That's what's making him so loopy and disjointed," Fiona observed.

Dona touched her fingers to the raw corners of his mouth. "Tell me what's going through your head, Nathan. Is she right? Is it all just the rush?"

"No," he said with sudden fierceness. "You think... You look around and think, why can't I feel like them? Laugh like them. You only feel when you hurt someone. That just makes you want to hurt the next one even more." He strangled on a harsh laugh. "How are you doing this to me? A spell? This place?"

"The way you desire to hurt others is a drug. You have to give it up to find what you really want," she replied softly. "You have to face what caused you to become addicted to it in the first place. That means you need to stop talking in third person and face yourself."

He stared at her and she waited, watching his mind process her words. "Once you do that, what's left?" he asked at last.

She found her voice suddenly not steady, as the look in his eyes took her back to a place she didn't want to go. "You may find there's nothing left. Nothing real."

He closed his eyes. "This pain...is clean. Do it all over again, Mistress. Over and over, again and again. The way you hurt me...it's different. Just keep hurting me like that and maybe that will become what's real."

The trembling in his hand increased, the stress overtaking him. Fiona might think he was incoherent, but every word made too much sense to Dona. He made her ache. Reaching up, she closed her hand on his forearm, holding her grip there to steady him. How could she not, when the painful perplexity and the rage warring in his heart were making her heart break? She'd hoped she didn't have a heart anymore.

"I like you adorned like this for me. I like you suffering for me. But I have plans for you." The indifference she summoned up in her own eyes almost faltered before the uncertainty in his, because it pierced straight through the block of ice around her heart. "So now I'll take all the pain away as I promised. The bad kind of pain."

Feeling his hand slide naturally to a place at the back of her neck under her hair, she leaned forward over his left nipple. He tensed, his fingers curling, but he did not impede her as she closed her mouth over the tender area.

Nathan sucked in a breath and then released it, his eyes widening as her tongue laved the jewel, the abused nipple. She knew the raw, throbbing pain had disappeared at the touch of her mouth, replaced with heightened sexual intensity that nipples experienced once the piercing was well healed. His ragged breath spoke of pleasure instead of pain as she continued to nibble on him, nuzzle, tug on the loop. When he grunted in distress, she saw his cock had started to rise, those piercings not having had the benefit of the healing agents in her mouth. She moved with leisurely deliberation to the other nipple, attending him there, watching him alternately squirm and writhe. Heard him curse as the pain of his cock warred with the pleasure she was providing his nipples.

Dona moved down his belly. Tracing her tongue over each of those well-cut stomach muscles, enjoying the taste of his hot, smooth skin, she summoned the organic bindings to shorten the tether on his arms, so that she moved out of the range of his touch. She saw his hands dig into the grass as her breath touched his erection. When he groaned, it made her wet. Wetter. The power of giving him so much pleasure and pain at once made her feel almost drunk with it. She wanted to nuzzle and torment him for hours, see and feel that body buck, hear his voice cry out for her, plead. Blowing on him, she watched the red skin fade. As the bruises vanished, she stroked her tongue up that ladder. He uttered an animal sound. She sampled his pre-cum trickling down his rigid staff, the flavor mixed with surgical steel, the residue of blood and musky skin.

"Mercy, Mistress. God, please..."

She had no interest in mercy now that she had his taste, his heat in her mouth. She wanted to ride him, feel that ring that had pierced the thin skin of the urethra flick against her inside like moth wings while the ladder stroked her with the primitive roughness she liked. She wanted to pull on his nipple rings as she rode him, see him flinch. Have him hoarsely beg her to let him come, let his hard cock spurt into her, bathing her with heat where she'd been cold so long.

She loved his eyes. How evil could grow in a soul that shone so beautifully through those blue irises, she couldn't begin to understand. His blond brows were thickly feathered, low, so the deep set of his eyes beneath them gave him a depth of intensity that could pull her inside him. Though she saw many things she didn't like there, there were shades of other things hiding in the dark jungle his soul had become, asking to be saved. Asking her to bring in light and make the blue sparkle with the facets of precious gems. A light that could drive out his demons and help *her* forget.

She stilled abruptly. She couldn't forget. That was a crazy thought. How could she erase a pain so intense she'd wanted to stop breathing?

"Something I can do for you, Mistress?"

She looked back toward his face. In the light of the sun, fanned by the shadow of the palm fronds rustling in the breeze above them she caught it, just the barest flicker. Calculation. The evil had felt her coming. It was whispering in his ear that the vulnerability she was demonstrating through her desire was giving him the upper hand, that soon he would have control. Control was the most important thing.

It was as Lucifer had said. Nathan had so far to go. It wasn't like the movies, where in two hours a person could change his life around. Save the world, get the girl. Live happily ever after.

It made her angry at him, at Lucifer, at herself. She'd let down her guard because he was her other half. Soul mates. Romantic, mortal nonsense that had turned out to be cosmically true. She felt sure that it was true specifically to bedevil her in a place that had plenty of devils and demons already.

She rose, towering over him, knowing it would increase his sense of helplessness and subjugation to her.

"The pain's breaking you down," she observed with a coolness not matched by the fire roiling in her blood. A fire that demanded she take him into her body as much as it demanded that she scream at him, hurt him. "I can't believe you fooled so many women. Now I understand the arrogance and the confidence you keep trying to exercise even here, in a place where your every action is transparent. Work a bitch on Earth, work a bitch in Hell, what does it matter? We can all be played." She bent, making sure he couldn't help but be tortured by the sight of her breasts trembling above the tight hold of her corset. She slid one long fingernail through the ring on his left nipple.

He was a hard-core Mistress's dream, aroused by pain and torment, hungering for the contrast of a tender touch at unexpected moments. She could see that sweet, submissive part of his soul so clearly that he could not. For the other souls she'd redeemed, having that clarity had been a roadmap to the final destination. With him, it was the shine of gold treasure, obliterating the path entirely. She just wanted to make him serve her. Keep him forever. Torture and tease him, bring him to climax in ways he couldn't even imagine.

His lips curled back from his teeth as she tugged hard enough to make him arch up against the pain. She held him that way, his upper torso in a crescent that he had to hold unless he wanted the ring torn out. "With one blink—" She closed her lashes, reopened them and watched his expression transform from discomfort to outright agony as she brought back the raw pain of the newly done piercings. When she blinked again, he froze, his expression confused as the pain vanished just as quickly. "I can make everything change for you. I'm running the orchestra here. You'll sing and play exactly as I wish.

"Our lives are lives of self-illusion, Jonathan. We create mirrors, surround ourselves with them. Those mirrors hide the real images of our lives, of who we are." As she brought her face even closer, she could tell he didn't know whether to be fascinated by her proximity or terrified. "When you were under the water before, when they were bathing you, what mirror did you see?"

"What?" The confusion increased. "Mirror, I didn't see—"

"Who did you see?" She twisted hard, her finger now threaded through that D-ring up past the first knuckle. The nipple screwed into a smaller point. Even as his upper body stayed as still as possible for his self-preservation, his hips bucked the small amount allowed against his restraints.

Oh yes. It made her throb, watching the fascinating fight between his soul's desire to give her everything, surrender totally, and his frightened ego's attempt to hold on to control. She could imagine the way he would beg if his soul won. The way his blue eyes would fire with lust, those hard muscles straining, just for her. Her name a gasp on his lips, his cock hard inside her, driving deeper as she urged him on. He'd talk dirty to her, say things to make her come, because she'd get absorbed in watching the words form on his perfect lips.

Her anticipation was too sharp, interfering with her focus. She needed to release her tension, or at least spill some of the boiling water out of the pot to keep it from overflowing altogether. Well, why not? There was no rule against it, though it was something she'd never done with her assignments before. It was going to shock Fiona and the others. The moment she gave herself permission for it regardless, a hard shudder went through her.

"We'll go back to the question later. You think about it."
She released him abruptly, straightening. "Right now, I'm
going to fuck you."

# Chapter Six

**ʂ໑**

Nathan couldn't keep up with her. Couldn't follow one thought before she had him chewing on another. The mirror reference brought back that hated face below the water, but Dona drove that and everything else away with that one electrifying announcement. Since she'd come back, there was a feverish quality to her that made him wonder what had happened. Who she'd met and why she seemed to have a razor-sharp edge of hunger honing her words, her touch.

She spun in a circle, loosing her hair. As she did, the clothes she wore melted away like paint, running in sensual rivers down the curves of her body before vanishing into the grass beneath her feet with no evidence of their passage. Now she was as naked as he was. So different, though. So many soft and wonderful places where he was hard.

There were those who said a woman was sexier in scanty clothes than she was completely naked. They'd never seen Dona. Lush was the perfect word. Heavy breasts, tiny waist, generous hips that flared out, telling him her ass would be worth begging to see. Her legs, while not long, were toned and slender, making him imagine how snugly she'd hold him while he fucked her. If he could get up, he'd lift her, slam her up against a palm tree and just bury himself inside that wet pussy.

She'd been playing so much with his head, this switching of gears was like a gift from God. When she stepped back over him and simply lowered herself onto his cock, he realized he'd never truly known what a gift was.

God...the sensation... He'd heard how men's piercings increased a woman's pleasure, but he hadn't realized how much more sensitive it would make him. His fury with her taunting, with her ability to shoot down his best attempts to gain the advantage on her, all of that receded at the joining of their two bodies. He willed more blood into his cock to make it harder, thicker so he could feel the full pressure of the clamp of her silken walls on him. The restraint over his hipbones did not give him control in any way. It was all her, coming down on him at her own pace, her small hands braced on his upper abdomen.

*Yes. This is where I want to be.* Experiencing her in all his senses, being with her in every way. Taking care of her forever so she'd never want anyone else.

He told himself Fiona was right, his response came from the endorphins of the piercings. Or the weirdness of this place Dona called Hell.

He'd never thought about taking care of a woman. Not...for a long time. If he did think about it, it was part of a strategy. Opening doors, getting them a drink... It was a form of caring for a woman even Mistresses enjoyed, for it was evidence that the slave liked serving their needs. He looked at Dona's hands braced on his stomach to balance herself, the fragile slim fingers curling in as she sought her pleasure. He thought of the pain and tiredness he'd seen just for a moment in her face when she'd returned from her mysterious meeting. It bothered him. He wanted to...

"Please, Mistress." The words came from a part of himself he didn't know. "Please release my hips so I can serve you properly."

She studied his face as she went down on him another inch, her fingers digging in even more. She was tight, so blessedly tight. "Please, Mistress."

The bonds slid away and his hips were free. Miraculously, so were his hands. He wanted so much to put them on her, but he waited, wondering at the tremors that ran through his body as she wrapped her delicate fingers around each wrist and guided his hands to her bare hips.

"Not until I come," she reminded him. He heard the catch in her voice as she sank down further. He tightened his hands on her, rising to meet her in the same motion.

"Never," he promised, though he was already setting his teeth against that increased sensitivity, the stroke of her on the ladder. After five years in prison, he should have gone off like a rocket at the slick glove of her pussy. Hell, he should have spewed the moment she stood up on the seat of her car. He didn't know if he was aided by his otherworldly surroundings, but he called on the same discipline he'd used to keep himself from jacking off and clung to it grimly, even as his body shuddered. He wanted her to go first. He wanted to know he'd brought her to that pinnacle while buried deep inside her. He wanted to believe he'd given it to her with an intensity no other man had. She was his. His.

The thoughts were astonishing, but they flowed from his mind with the blurting, tumbling clumsiness of a man discovering prayer.

Jesus, it was Heaven and Hell both. As she rose and fell, he learned her preferred cadence, keeping his strokes steady, taking her deeper with the strength in his hands. It gave him an unexpected humble gratitude, the ability to offer her something she didn't have herself. Vibrators could bring sensation, but they couldn't duplicate the feel of a man's hands, demanding, desiring her, cherishing her skin so she'd know being with her was better to him than a widescreen TV, a sports car or front-row tickets to the Superbowl.

Her breasts moved before him, swaying, wobbling. He couldn't help his mouth.

"You've got the most beautiful breasts I've ever seen."

He wanted to bury his face in them, suckle them. Be smothered in them. As if she heard the cry of his heart she pressed them to his face, curling her arms around his head as he drew up his now free legs to press his thighs against her ass and raised his hips to accommodate the new angle. His adjustment earned him a soft cry from her lips, brushing his ear. He clutched a generous handful of each buttock and plunged in harder, increasing his stroke length even as his mouth found a nipple, latched on and suckled with ferocity. God, if she didn't go over, he was going to explode. He'd almost welcome that damn cock harness now to make sure he stayed in check just long enough.

Her cheek pressed against his bare crown, her breath coming hard. She was strong, lithe, matching him movement for movement. The pleasure was almost as unbearable as the pain had been.

"If this is Hell, I want to stay forever," he groaned.

At the words, she shattered, bowing back, putting her breast deeper into his mouth. Tugging, tormenting, he kept up the stimulation as the pressure of her fingers increased against his head. He wondered if she was wishing that she'd left him his hair so she could yank on it. He missed it too, a woman's way of using his hair to communicate her urgency, affection or nurturing... Her cunt convulsed against him, clutching at his cock with squeezing, excoriating pressure as she climaxed, making him groan.

*Don't come. Don't come until she says you can. That's the way it works.* Her hand whispered across his scalp, making him think of her stroking it when it had hair. He seized on the image to steady him, imagined himself with her in a park, his head in her lap as she petted him, read a book. Slowly, lazily tangling her fingers in the locks. Putting him to sleep, even as his cock stirred, thinking of her touch moving down...

Up until now he'd never thought of his hair or any feature of his body as anything more than an indication of how well he was doing at giving his Mistress the kind of pleasure she wouldn't want to do without. No matter how often he dangled it before her and drew it away. A delicate game of cat and mouse he'd played where the Mistress eventually became an emotionally dependent slave. Now there was only Dona and the pleasure he'd created for her, the cries coming from her throat, the bite of her nails and the soft slap of her slick body against his. Though she'd said where the finish line was, he wanted her permission to let go. If he came inside her, it would be the height of intimacy, an avenue into her soul, a way to connect she couldn't deny. He was sure of it. It was in his grasp, like the glint of a hard metal trophy.

"Mistress," he rasped, still pumping hard, his voice muffled somewhat by her round curves, his mouth hot and wet on the valley between those quivering breasts. "Please... Let me come for you."

He was so close, bursting with it, so it took a moment to register her response, the fact she was drawing away, rising off his cock, even as his body bucked.

"No."

"No—" He couldn't help himself. His hands reached out to seize her hips, to yank her back. All the pain of the piercings and the burn of the earlier rape by Fiona slammed back into him full force, overpowering him. Because he'd learned to have fast reflexes in prison, he held her fast anyway, gritting his teeth. He was going to come inside her, dammit. He was going to break into her head even if he had to do it with force.

The grass restraints reared out of the ground, coiled around his wrists and wrenched his arms out to either side of him, tearing his hands from her. They looped over and over to hold him up to the armpits. He struggled, trying to get away, but the other restraints were back as well, anchoring his waist and hips, holding him still, agonizingly on the brink of orgasm. The pain was gone like a passing thought and the denied release tore at him with savage, lustful teeth.

The image of them in the park vanished. He would have murdered her if he was free. Hurt her as she'd just deliberately hurt him. But that's what women did. Had he forgotten so quickly? She was a cleverer Mistress than he'd given her credit for. She'd blindsided him and he felt the impact as if his soul had collided with a diesel truck. He'd been trying to give her everything, hadn't he? What the hell did she want?

"Conniving cunt," he snarled. "Damn you."

The look in her eyes was brittle, withdrawn. The traces of mortal woman were gone, replaced with a creature that was seductress, otherworldly and dangerous. "Been there, done that, Jonathan. Why do you think I'm here?"

She cocked a brow, her gaze passing over the ladder and D-ring, a reminder that she had ways of tethering him in almost any way she desired. While it made him angry and fearfully anxious, he also stayed powerfully aroused.

"What the hell have you done to me? No matter what you do, my dick just wants you more."

She knelt beside him, her knee brushing his hip as she reached out and toyed with one of the nipple rings. His cock leaked fluids. If she touched him there at all, he was sure he'd go off like a geyser. She studied his turgid member, an absorbed expression on her face. Despite his rage with her, he couldn't help but be distracted by the delicate angles of her profile, so at odds with the strength that pulsed from her like roaring flame.

"It's because you *are* a male submissive, Nathan," she said at last, bringing her gaze back to his. "You don't like to admit it to yourself, but you didn't jack off in prison once, did you? What kind of man does that? What kind of man feels he can't allow himself satisfaction unless a woman commands it?"

His lip curled, wanting to deny it, but she wasn't done. "You're a submissive of such wondrous beauty and power, any Mistress would kill to cherish you as her own. If your soul wasn't poisoned. And if you weren't mine."

The possessive comment startled him, the proprietary words slamming into his chest, robbing him of breath for a moment. When he remembered how she'd left him dangling, so close to coming, he rallied.

"Was that what denying me was about? Your way of 'cherishing' me?" He sneered it.

"Karma has a much shorter turnaround time here. Wasn't that what you were doing to me a few moments ago? Bringing me pleasure and then planning to use it against me as a weapon?"

"I was right," he snarled. "To try to do it to you before you did it to me." He yanked against the bonds. With her words rasping across his nerve endings, his limbs jerked as if they'd been touched by electrical current. He was feeling suffocated. He had to go, to leave. He needed to run.

"Sshh...ssshh..." When she touched his head to calm him, he whipped in that direction, seized her wrist in his teeth and bit down.

He punctured her flesh, clamping his jaws together with the grim determination of a pit bull. She'd know he wasn't to be fucked with. Play with his mind, would she? Bitch. She wasn't allowed to hurt him. No woman hurt him.

*No, no woman will. If you could reach my face, would you tear that away too? Break my ribs, rip them free, gnaw on them? Will consuming the flesh and heart of a woman give you your vengeance on us? Bring you peace?*

The red haze before his eyes began to fade away at the gruesome image of himself bathed in blood and reveling in it. Wanting nothing more than to kill anything female. Dona wasn't struggling. She hadn't cried out. He could taste her blood, but she was sitting motionless, letting him hold her arm in that bear trap grip, her dark eyes watching him.

She could feel pain. That at least was a relief, something familiar. There was a tension to her features, a quiver in her wrist against his cheek. It bothered him though, seeing those signs of pain but no signs of her trying to strike out at him. She lifted her other hand, touched his cheek.

"Jonathan has made you into a rabid animal, hasn't he? Nothing but rage. Ssshhh... Let me go, my sweet slave. Let me go."

As he eased his bite, her fingers wiped away the blood on his lips, even as her arm oozed more, dripped onto his skin. It gave him back that image of being bathed in her blood. He swallowed, tasting it in a way that made bile rise in his stomach. No. He didn't want that.

"You're a submissive naturally," she said softly. "You've made yourself a vicious bottom. On top of that, you have the territorial instincts of an alpha. All those facts don't change anything. You've never trusted yourself to experience being a submissive fully, or met the woman who can force you to do so. Until now. You stay here a moment and think."

As if he had any choice. Rising, she walked down to the water's edge, dipping her arm in the sparkling current. When she lifted it, blood and teeth marks were gone, but he felt as if the wound was still there, evidenced by the way she turned her back on him, leaving him bound and ignored.

When she sat down on the bank, he followed her gaze to where Fiona was bathing. Her leopard sat restively on the bank. When Olivia joined Fiona in the water, she poured liquid from one of those crystal bottles over her breasts. Fiona massaged the soap in, enjoying her own touch, apparently unconcerned by their regard. As Olivia let the bottle drift away in the water, she pressed herself against Fiona's back, her hands moving forward to help as Fiona let out a sigh of pleasure and leaned against her, nestling her head comfortably and looking up at the blue sky, the froth of clouds moving overhead. Most of the other women were in the water now too. Playing with each other or floating on their backs like sensually curved lily pads, their pale breasts the white blooms. Dona linked her hands around her bent knees. She was still naked, her hair whispering down her pale back.

Sirens, just like the picture. Only in this quiet moment when they weren't concerned with him, he thought he might be seeing the picture when Hylas wasn't in it. Not creatures of predatory danger to men, but women indulging their own pleasure in a quiet way, at ease in their surroundings and methods.

His attention was quickly jerked away as a hand took hold of his cock. He tried to jump back from Aliyah since the hand she gripped him with held her snake. The beast, a good foot of his body wrapped around her forearm, had his hooded head resting on the top of the hand that deftly snapped a tether on the new ring at the head of his cock.

"Get that..." He gritted his teeth, fighting the quivering panic that came from having very little ability to move. With that damn snake too close, he was afraid it would strike, be on his cock...

"Be still," Dona ordered. She'd turned, her head cocked as she watched them, her hair blowing across her shoulder, feathering against her left breast. He could see the pink lips of her pussy because the soles of her feet were spread apart, bracing her against the grass. She still glistened with her arousal, with his pre-cum.

While he didn't have much choice but to obey Dona's wishes, he couldn't help the futile locking of his muscles as Aliyah attached a second, shorter chain on her tether to the D-ring at the scrotum. The chain that had been installed with the piercing that ran the length of the ladder already put a strain on his constantly stiff cock. Now this tether attached to the crown and root would join the equation, such that he'd be alternately teased and tormented by any increase in his erection or fiercely administered yank.

After Dona's refusal to allow him release he wanted to put his own hands defiantly on his cock. He could have jerked off to climax in probably less than ten seconds, as long as natural body function still worked as it should here. He could tell himself that doubt caused his hesitation, but it seemed like the tunnel through which he'd always seen the writing of his thoughts had expanded, a light cast on a jumble of different theories he hadn't wanted or thought of considering.

Did he want to have Dona command his release to prove he could hold out for it? Or because he wanted to know she desired it, like when he was eating her cunt? Or maybe she'd hit the right nerve, saying that he had a true submissive's nature, that something inside him needed her to command it?

Bullshit. It was all bullshit. He could think straight if Aliyah would pull that damn snake back a few feet. Okay, a fucking mile wouldn't be far enough. He turned his gaze away from the creature, knowing the ridiculous but overwhelming compulsion to keep staring at the serpent would not keep fangs from sinking into his flesh. He focused on Dona and tried to figure out something that would transfer some of the power back to his side.

She was sitting on that bank like an innocent girl, for Christ's sake. She had a mole on the back of one thigh, a tiny scrape on one finger from who knew what. Did they have Band-Aids in Hell? Little demons with red faces and horns printed on them, like kid's bandages? Her mouth, when relaxed in neither smile nor frown as it was now, was somewhat crooked on her face.

Unfortunately, that curvy little body, those wet crooked lips, the dark, taunting eyes, the memory of all of that rising and falling over him, was not helping in the least. He cursed on a groan as Aliyah gave him a cruelly playful squeeze before she stepped back. The restraints on his limbs vanished, releasing him at the same moment that damned snake's tongue flickered against his skin. He scrambled back and swore even more colorfully as he came to the end of Aliyah's firmly held chain. The resulting pain brought to mind the disturbing memory from his childhood social studies class, where he saw Richard Harris suspended by his pectorals in *A Man Called Horse*. He shuddered.

Dona rose then, sauntering toward him. The innocence vanished and the boots reappeared. He watched the first sway of her hips as she moved toward him in nothing but those boots. Then the latex pants slithered up her legs, repainting her pussy and hips. The corset closed around her, cinching up and lifting her breasts so that the swivel of her hips became even more pronounced. When she put out her hand, Aliyah laid the end of the tether over it. Dona twitched it idly, so he felt the movement like electrical current running between the scallops of chain connecting each ladder down to the scrotum ring. There were three feet between them and he ached to close the distance, just slide his arms around her and find out how she would feel in his arms. Maybe she'd like it, like knowing he was strong and could hold her as long as she wanted him to do so. The thought made his heart ache in an unusual way, not necessarily pleasant. For some reason that didn't matter. He didn't want to stop feeling that desire.

As if she'd read his thoughts, his Mistress spoke. "Hands behind your back."

He made himself stand still this time, keeping his eyes on hers. Watched hers heat at his obedience.

It was Olivia who came out of the water, droplets rolling down her breasts, her hair shiny and wet on her bare shoulders. She cuffed his wrists to the crooks of his elbows so his arms were folded up above the small of his back again. Dona stood before him while it was done, twisting the leash.

"Lower your eyes."

"No."

When she reached out to brush at his lashes and force his compliance, he turned his head, pressed his lips to that spot on her arm, the one that no longer bore the imprint of his teeth. He brushed his cheek against her. *I'm sorry.* He couldn't say the words, but hoped she felt them.

She stayed still, let him do it. He lowered his eyes then.

"Are you ready to obey your Mistress?" She murmured it. There was something wistful to the tone, something that was an odd echo of what he'd just felt in his own heart.

He inclined his head. He felt as if he were gripped by a fever as he stood before her so helpless and aroused at once.

Was this what those male subs felt, the married ones, the ones with Mistresses to whom they'd committed themselves entirely, permanently collared? This feral, raging desire to do or be anything she wished, if only she'd keep them chained to her side forever?

It was a disturbing thought, such that he couldn't help hesitating as Dona turned and began to walk away, expecting him to follow. She glanced back at him.

"Keep it up and I'll shove a dildo as big as Fiona's strap-on back up your ass to keep your mind where it should be. You'll shuffle along behind me like an old man."

That galvanized him into motion, despite his upper lip curling in a rebellious sneer she acknowledged with a half-smile and a sharp tug. He followed, for he didn't want his ass stretched like that again. The memory of the pain was far too vivid to ignore.

When he took two steps after her, the oasis was gone. He blinked in semi-darkness. Flashing lights and heavy metal music pounded through the soles of his feet. Bodies were on all sides of him dancing, turning, bumping. Sweat, perfumes, aftershaves, the smell of sex and excitement. He was in a nightclub, a fetish club apparently, for those around him were in various BDSM wear, though he was the only one he could see that was completely naked. It made him self-conscious, more so as all eyes turned toward him, male and female, enjoying the show. Suddenly the mob of people made room, putting him inside a clear circle of space for as many as possible to see him so subjugated before his Mistress. Naked, shaved and pierced, tied to her with a leash, his arms bound behind him in a way that he could be booted off balance with a shove.

"I don't like this," he said in a hoarse voice. There was no way she could hear him over the noise, but of course her eyes were on him and she seemed to understand. She wrapped the chain around her fist, tugged. He sucked in a breath, took a step forward.

"You'll dance for me, now. Move that fine ass."

When he shook his head, she wrapped another length around her fist. Deliberately raising her arm into the air, she drew up the slack, taking him to his toes as she pulled on his scrotum. His swelling cock was pulled down in a curve by the limits of the scallops of chain connecting the ladder barbells.

"Jesus…"

"You can dish it out, but you can't take it? Remember Mistress Narcissa?" Dona's voice resounded in his head, an insidious whisper impossible to shut out. "You danced with her on a club floor like this one. You'd been hers and hers alone for several months. On a slow song, she pressed you to your knees, her eyes full of you, her soul open. Every eye turned to watch, sensing that something important was about to happen, something worth watching. She laid her hand on your shoulder, caressed your nape with her fingers. Whispered, 'I love you'."

He knew what was coming, but he couldn't look away from the dark truth in Dona's gaze. "You looked up at her a full moment without saying anything. Slowly, the eyes she'd always seen focused on her in adoration and obedience transformed to an expression of triumph and scorn. You spat in her face, laughed at her. Then you rose and left her there on the floor by herself."

Dona's eyes glittered, her lips thinning.

"So dance."

A sharp barb stung his flank. Nathan spun as much as he was able to do so. Another Mistress stood on the outer edges, tall, an Amazon. Her female submissive crouched at her feet, watching him and Dona. She wore a collar and leash the Amazon held in her free hand. That leash had a second chain that connected to a navel and clit piercing revealed by her transparent body stocking. The arrangement would give the big woman a similar control over her sub to that which Dona had over him.

The Amazon had struck him with a long buggy whip. As he turned, she did it again, stinging his erection.

He cried out from the pain. Dona brought a whip she now had in her right hand into play, striking his thigh so he shifted it, pulling on the other side of his leash so he hopped that way. He spun as the other Mistress struck him again. He was dancing like a puppet between them, the artful tugs of the cock tether and skillful placement of the whips making him perform a lurching shuffle, awkward with his arms bound. Those surrounding jeered at him while eyeing his stiff cock appreciatively and making crude comments.

Punishment from a Mistress, from Dona, he could take. This was different. He was horrified to feel tears stinging his eyes. Blinking them back, he kept up the dance.

*You're not supposed to betray those you love.*

*But you betrayed those who loved you…*

His gaze rose, despite his intense desire to keep his eyes down. In the crowd, waiting for him, he saw all of his past Mistresses, almost a full dozen.

Narcissa, Lady Jane, Melinda…even the murderess who had put him here, though he tried not to look at her. Every one of them was there…except Lauren. All beautiful women, well-cared for, self-assured.

The shadows of his past haunting him. They were not jeering. While he wondered why Lauren was missing, he was grateful that she was, for all of them just stared at him silently with the expressions they'd had when he had shown them his true face. His moment of victory. That moment that said, "You thought you had my love. I never needed you. I'll never depend on any of you. You'll never make me a fool."

They spun around him as if he was the fulcrum of a merry-go-round that had gotten knocked off its pin, lurching him in a spiraling motion he couldn't predict. His throat was tight, his chest aching, and he didn't know why.

*Pain is a mirror. You weren't content until everything was a mirror of your own pain.*

He was beyond questioning how Dona could speak in his head as easily as he could talk to her with his lips. He tried to turn away, but they were on all sides, backing him into the center of the circle again.

*Why did you do it, Jonathan? What's the face in the mirror? The final one, behind everything else?*

"Stop." He shouted it, trying to get away from those faces and find Dona. She had to be at the end of the leash, but he couldn't see her. A crowd of strangers pressed in on him now, invasive hands on his cock, his ass, playing with the nipple rings. A tongue at his scrotum, fingers pushing between his buttocks as his legs were held by multiple hands. Lifting him up like a rag doll with no control of his own actions. Goading his lust and his fear as he struggled, his body vibrating toward an orgasm that he didn't want, a violation like rape.

"Dona, please…"

*Stripped, nowhere to hide…you've been there before. Why did you forget what it was like? Why would you do this to someone else?*

"You're not supposed to do this to me!" He screamed into the roar of club noise which swallowed his protest like a monstrous beast, making it insignificant. Not even a whisper among the din. "You're not supposed to do this to me…" *Not to someone you love.*

*You're so right. So why did you?*

With each of them, a part of him had craved something he couldn't dare to want. It had gotten worse and worse with each game, each Mistress. He felt it now, looking at them.

*But what about Mistress Lauren? Why isn't she there?* Dona's voice, mocking him.

*You're controlling this. You should know.* He shot the thought back to her resentfully. Desperately. *I don't want to talk about Lauren.*

*We will. Not now, but we will. You felt something for all of your Mistresses, but especially her, because she reminded you of someone…*

"No, stop it!" He started to struggle and kick, fighting the hands on him, not caring who he struck, just so long as they let go. It was futile. The more he convulsed in their grip, the greater their laughter and cruelty became. Their hands became more brutal, stretching him, thrusting, pinching. His upper body was dropped so his legs were higher in the air, allowing someone's tongue to tease his anus behind, his cock in front. At eye level he saw a man's cock approaching, enormous and adorned with a spiked shield piercing, sharp metal tips that would cut when the organ was thrust brutally into a vulnerable mouth. Despite all of these frightening things, nothing was worse than that laughter. He needed the laughter to stop.

*Surrender. Just surrender.*

*Not to them. Never. Not to anyone…*

*Even me, your true Mistress? The one who knows who you are, everything that lies within your heart? Every hope you've had, every dream you've destroyed because you didn't dare to believe in hope?*

Her words wove around him like a net, inexorably immobilizing his limbs, taking away his will to fight. Surrender…

Surrender to his Mistress. He could do that, couldn't he? He knew there were reasons not to do so, but he didn't want to hear those voices. It didn't matter anymore. They could defile him and it would mean nothing. He was nothing. Going limp in all those hands, he let them do what they would. He was just an object anyway. Something nobody wanted, even himself. It was an unexpected thought, but as that huge dick came toward him, the acrid smell of bloodstained metal approaching his lips, it all made sense.

*There you are. Nathan. That's who I want. Not Jonathan.*

The others melted away, returning to their couplings and dancing. He was standing again and Dona was there. Cupping her hands around his bound forearms at the small of his back, she pressed herself to him. Her hips, lower abdomen and pubic mound were against his arousal. Her thighs caressed the sensitive tip, the movement of her body sliding the D-ring back and forth.

"Dance with me."

This he could do. Sway with her, let her grip steady and guide him as she shifted her weight to a poignant song. The lead singer crooning that he wanted to kiss the eyelids of his sleeping lover and never leave the world of dreams with her. He didn't want it to end.

Of course. Only Aerosmith could provide the proper soundtrack for Hell.

"Just dance with me. Don't think."

His Mistresses' faces still stared at him from among the crowd around them. Their eyes were everywhere the strobe lights were, eyes glowing in the dark.

Dona's palms caressed the upper curve of his buttocks. He dipped his head, pressing his face against her hair. "There are so many of them," she observed in a whisper. He squeezed his eyes shut, but the words kept coming. He wished he could touch her, but she had everything. The right to touch him, cup him as she did now, bringing one hand between them to arouse him even as she punished him with her voice. "In the end, you wanted the next one even before you were done with the previous Mistress. You were getting desperate, too hungry. So at last you chose a Mistress who could destroy you. Put an end to your hunger."

The S&M Killer had been described that way. The bloodlust driving her mad so she took her victims faster and faster, until she made the fatal step. He shook his head, tried to pull back, but the cock leash and Dona held him fast. "No. I wasn't like her."

"In that way, you were. See your Mistresses another way. Open the eyes of your soul like a newborn. Have the bravery of an infant to face the reality with no blinders on to protect yourself. I know you can. I know you have courage."

Because she believed he could, he found himself raising his head, lifting his nose from her hair to look at them. They were illuminated in the crowd, motionless among the many gyrating bodies so he could not miss them. Silent, accusatory statues. Compassionate women who had loved him, sexy Mistresses confident in their power who never expected his intention was to shred and throw their love back into their faces.

No, he didn't want these thoughts. These weren't his. That wasn't how it was. They had malice in them, they all did. If he hadn't done it to them, they'd have done it to him. Eventually.

His gaze flicked down so he could stare into Dona's face. Desperately he sought it, that trace of deception he saw lurking in every woman's eyes. Her eyes, dark and mysterious, were capable of hiding everything. But as they looked back into his, all he felt was confusion clouding what he'd always believed to be true.

Another body pressed against his back. Two hands slid up his thighs, teasing the muscles and the curve of his buttocks. Aliyah and her snake.

"How long does this go on?" He couldn't stop himself from asking the child's question.

"Until I say so. Until you figure it out." Dona answered the question as Aliyah's hands caressed his biceps. Dona palmed the broadness of his back. The snake woman's purr of pleasure and warm breath were against his spine.

"You can't fool me," his Mistress whispered. "You can't run." Her fingers crept up to his nape as Aliyah's lips pressed just below that portion of his skin. Their bodies held him between them, soft, generous curves of breast, hip and the lengths of their thighs against him. The strain on the piercings as his large erection increased proportionately made his head light, just as Dona had predicted. He tried to look away from the knowledge in Dona's face, but he couldn't.

"You thought you discovered the ultimate game preserve in the BDSM scene. Mistresses who have the audacity to bring a man to his knees willingly, for his own pleasure and theirs. You thought you were the hunter, but we both know there was more than that going on, don't we?" She rubbed her thighs against him, captured his cock between them and let him feel the pressure of her pussy on top of him, the squeeze of her thighs. "I could make you come just from this. Because you've always wanted your true Mistress, the one who will care for your soul, the part that needs her so desperately. A Mistress you could love and cherish fully with no fear of her betrayal. Jonathan is keeping you from that."

"Maybe he protects me from the empty fantasy. The lie of it. Aren't *you* here because you don't believe in it?"

He'd lashed out defensively, but he saw he'd landed an arrow with that one. He felt satisfaction along with a moment of regret at the flash of pain through her expression. He shoved it away. "Fuck you. You're just playing with my head, like all of them."

Her lips tightened, her eyes going cool. "I'm trying to get you to stop listening to your fucked-up head and listen to your heart. If you want to do it rough, we can do it rough." She stepped back, taking her body beyond his reach, her attention shifting to his shoulder.

What he'd thought were Aliyah's hands moving to his shoulders was something else. Two snakes, one coming up over either side. He twisted, crying out in fear, but Dona had the chain to his cock still wrapped around her fist. At some point during her fondling, Aliyah apparently had snapped one to the back of the collar and tethered it to the arms, so all she had to do was keep her hand in that taut vertical line of chain to hold him fast. He struggled as more snakes came out of the mosaic floor at his feet and wound around his ankles, spiraling up his calves to his thighs, holding him the same way the pond weed and ropes of grass had done. Only these restraints moved, rasping their live, damp bodies against his skin. The snake at his right shoulder wound around his throat once and then continued down his body, the slender body perfectly suited to winding herself in a tight coil along the length of his cock, giving him a momentary terror as to whether boa constrictors came in pencil-width size. However, the snake seemed content to hover just above his genitals, the threat somehow worse than the reality.

He'd immediately assumed the creature was a she, as if a threat to his manhood could only come in female form. Wouldn't Dona have a field day with that one? He wished he was flaccid and limp so he could dissuade the creature from using his cock as a tree limb. However, whether it was the piercings, the curse of the place or Dona's presence commanding him, his traitorous body was more attuned to her Will than his sense of self-preservation. He remained hard as a steel rod.

"Now, my arrogant slave." Dona reached out, her fingernails raking down his chest, caressing him and the snakes together. "Stay very still for me. Not a muscle, except those I want you to move."

The crowd was a shifting, blurred movement of shadows outside their circle now. Even the music had died to a mumbling roar of sound, like a distant ocean. Olivia stepped to her side holding a box. Nathan watched, fear turning his vital organs to ice. He had fucking snakes on him. All over him.

When Olivia opened the box for Dona, his Mistress withdrew the contents carefully. He knew he didn't want to look, but of course he did.

For a moment, he thought it was a three-headed snake, a creature of the surrealism of this world. It didn't help that the snake on his left shoulder suddenly dropped down his pectoral, latching on to his nipple ring. He cried out, expecting to be bitten, but the creature remained where she was. The snake at his midriff looped back up to take the opposite nipple ring so he had her weight pulling downward on the right ring as the other snake pulled upward on the left, a tugging sensation on each piercing.

When he was able to focus through his terror, he saw the object from the box was in fact an object. It wasn't a snake. It did move like one, like liquid silver in the *Terminator* films in serpentine form. A phallus come to life, as if Dona charmed men's cocks or the simile of one the way a snake charmer made a snake rise out of a basket and dance. She certainly had no difficulty getting his cock to rise, no matter the circumstance.

Dona stroked the three-headed thing's glittering liquid skin. "This lovely device has one purpose. It's going to give me great pleasure to watch it fulfill it with you. Stay very, very still."

Dona held up her arm, the chain to his cock still wrapped around her knuckles. The object started to elongate, ratcheting up his terror. He started back, an instinctive reaction, but Aliyah, her snakes and Dona had too firm a grip upon him. It wrapped around her arm like the coiled bracelet of an Egyptian queen. The largest "head" of the thing led the way, the other two gliding along like a bent fork's tines at the back.

"Wh-What does it do?"

"The two smaller heads will lengthen about six inches and wrap around your balls. Stretch them, milk them. The main head will drive deep inside you and fuck your ass."

He wasn't certain what happened next, but several moments later, rational thought returned to find him coughing, panting, hoarse from screaming out and struggling against his live bonds, a panic attack so bad he had no grip on his emotions, no sense of the passage of time.

"No... No... Don't touch me with that." He was raging, pleading. His mind told him it wasn't a snake, that it was an inanimate object that was no different from a sex toy run on batteries, but the way they'd covered him with the real things took common sense away. It was just too much.

The snake bindings on his legs vanished, a momentary reprieve only as Dona and Aliyah shoved him up to the nightclub's bar. His upper body slammed down on the countertop. Dona held the back of his neck in one hand, the tether between his collar and arms drawn taut in the other, putting pressure on his windpipe. Now Aliyah had his cock leash as she kicked his legs more widely apart. The snakes from the floor returned, restraining him from ankle to thigh. He thought he could feel the flicker of the damn things' tongues at the base of his testicles.

"Hush. Tell me a slave's first responsibility." Dona's grip was merciless, her nails biting into his skin. "Tell me the answer, or it will get much worse."

He wanted to scream at her to let him go, but something penetrated his panic. Under her merciless hold, one of her fingertips was playing with the curve of his ear. Stroking it in a way that suggested if he'd had hair, she'd be curling it around her finger in a soothing, almost maternal way. When he managed to glance up at her face, his own pressed to the bar, he saw it in her eyes. She would take care of him, get him through this. He just had to trust her. He, who hadn't trusted a woman since he could barely walk away from one. Nothing about this situation suggested that should change. But as her finger stroked him, a liquid warmth like baby's milk spilled into his chest, down into his stomach, coating the panic with an odd reassurance.

*Surrender.*

"To submit to the Will of his Mistress." His body strained helplessly, his mind resisting the idea even as his heart fought to take hold of it. "Because it's your right to use me as you wish."

"Yes."

Why not surrender to her? After all, she seemed to know everything, anticipated every potential strategy to take control before he attempted to execute it. No, not entirely. She hadn't anticipated the words he'd lashed at her a few moments ago. He had the power to hurt her. Normally, that would have made him feel exultation, knowing he had a vulnerability to exploit. He wanted to know her vulnerabilities, didn't he?

Of course he did. But did he want to know the pathway to her soul to tear it apart or to dwell there, instead of inside himself? Would he find the sense of security there only hinted at by that tiny reassuring caress at his ear?

The left snake that held his nipple ring released it briefly to rethread herself through an eyebolt screwed into the surface of the bar and then reclamped on his D-ring. He felt the snake on the right do the same thing, which allowed Dona to ease her grip on his neck. He was firmly fastened to the wood now by his nipple rings.

"I'm afraid, Mistress." His anger was accomplishing nothing.

"I know that." Her lips touched his spine as he felt the two small tails of the thing wrap themselves around his testicles as she'd indicated. Shadows reflected back at him in the bar mirror. A large woman with a cruel face, piglike eyes that narrowed, calculated, deceived. He remembered the suffocating smell of her crotch as she'd pushed his face into it and crooned. *Such a pretty boy...*

He squeezed his eyes shut, ducked his head.

"I'm with you." Dona's voice.

*Even though I walk through the valley of the shadow of death, I will fear no evil...* Words he remembered from a brief time when he thought religion could provide him a safe haven. "You're not real. I can't believe in you."

He made it a statement, but it was a question, made flat by terror.

"I'm the only thing you have to believe in," his Mistress said.

The thick body of the main phallus slid away from his testicles, moving between his thighs and up toward its goal. Its skin felt oily, slick, as if it secreted lubrication in its fluid skin. He wondered what department of Hell was in charge of creating such fantastical animated instruments of torture. Shaking under Dona's touch, he felt her hands slide down to his buttocks, caress him.

"Relax for your Mistress."

As if that would happen with the vision of what was about to happen exploding in his head. Dona kissed the small of his back, near where the device was. As she had said, those moist, soft lips, her warm breath and gentle touch, were his only anchors amid terror.

*I'm the only thing you have to believe in.*

Somehow, he had to make himself unclench. It was going to happen whether he wanted it to or not. It was her Will and he didn't want to fight it. He wanted to please her.

Closing his eyes, he visualized her sitting on the bar. Twining her arms and legs around him, she put her hands on his hips, catching the belt loops of his jeans to playfully tug him closer, rub against his crotch. He'd kiss her, long and deep, burying his fingers into her hair as her mouth opened to him and she took him inside her in every way he'd ever wanted to be inside a woman. Ways he hadn't remembered wanting until a red Mercedes came over a hill.

Dona could plant thoughts in the minds of her assignments, but she typically wasn't given the ability to read their minds in full, vivid detail. So she knew it was Lucifer's diabolical decision that she could suddenly see these images in Nathan's head, feel them. His hands were on her, cradling her face as they kissed, his thumbs sweeping up her throat, his body pushing against her. Her lower body heated and strained for his, wanting him to thrust deep inside her, his breath whispering on her face, those blue eyes closer than the promise of Heaven's tranquil touch.

He was using a fantasy about her to obey her commands. It was impossible not to be aroused by that, not to be distracted by it.

*"Because it's your right to use me as you wish."* He'd known that part of the answer, but he didn't realize there was another part to it. *Because a Mistress takes care of her slave.* Because he could trust her to get him through anything, anything she devised to heighten his pleasure or, in this case, to force him to face things he didn't want to face.

She almost missed her cue when he took a deep breath and let it out, relaxing his muscles.

Her fingers still resting on the curve of one buttock, she guided the device's broad head to the proper position. His ass was already well-lubricated and conditioned by Fiona's earlier invasion, so it did not take much effort to get the phallus pushed through. When his body stiffened, she teased the opening with her fingertips. His thigh muscles were cords that stood out, encouraging her to rub her leg against his, move her hand up the middle of his back, tracing a path back down the spine. She wanted to lay down on him, curve her hips over his and add pressure to the invasion, as if it were attached to her body and she was fucking him, making him feel pleasure.

It gave her some interesting pictures and ideas, but it also warned her that she was getting too caught up in this. As a mortal Mistress, her focus could be on bringing him pleasure while she pleased herself. A Mistress of Redemption's goal was different. She needed to remember that.

*Stop fucking with my head, Lucifer.*

As the device went even deeper, Nathan jolted at the searing wave of arousal that stroked through him when the flexible substance went to work on the sensitive channel. It felt as if it was squeezing his prostate. The snakes at his nipples were increasing the strength of their tugs. Suddenly terror was mixed with spiraling, roaring, intense lust. He shuddered, his ass pumping against the side of the bar in a shameless humping he couldn't stop, his breath rasping hard out of him.

"Mercy, he has a fine ass," someone murmured near him. Perhaps Mariah. He didn't know. Dona had not let him come earlier, had driven him near insanity, and here she was doing it again, bringing him into a realm of sensation more intense than any orgasm he'd ever experienced. So close and yet he couldn't release, the vise of the two extensions on his balls and the cock harness keeping him helpless.

"Please, Mistress..." he begged. "Please let me come for you." No artifice or calculating, just raw male need, a growl of desire, incoherent words. Glasses on the bar shook, fell over as his frenetic movements became more powerful, the muscles in his thighs bunching as he slammed against the bar again and again.

Her hand brushed the opening to his ass, her hand wrapped around the body of the surreal sex toy, letting him feel how stretched he was, letting him feel her touch.

"God, please... Goddamn..." He pumped harder and several glasses tumbled to the floor, shattering as he wished to do.

"Now," she murmured at last, reaching beneath him to loosen the harness at the same moment the vise on his balls eased, even as the head deep inside increased the fervor of its stimulation.

He roared with the force of the climax that crashed over him. Hot seed jetted from his cock in such a thick stream it was almost painful, splashing against the side of the bar and onto his knees. Warm cum ran down his legs and over the bodies of the snakes on his thighs, making their slight movements on him even more slippery.

Even if her teasing hadn't goaded him to such a high pitch, his body had been ready for this for five long years, saving up. He came long and hard, groaning, continuing to pump against the wood as her touch goaded him, an aftershock almost as hard as the orgasm taking him as she gripped his buttocks in both hands and kneaded them as he moved. The way she would if he was driving into her, her arms wrapped around him...

As he came, as his release poured out of him, something else rose in him, an emotional response bound to the physical, the way that chain was bound to his cock.

"Please..." The pitiful supplication was coming out of his mouth, but he didn't know what he was begging for. Or maybe he did. Oblivion. Peace. A chance to go back to the beginning and become the person a Mistress would truly want, not one who crafted a way to use her. But he had no clue how to do or be anything else than what he was now. How did he exorcise or heal a part of himself that seemed beyond his control? A part that seemed stronger than any other part of himself?

# Chapter Seven

ℰ

The snakes were gone, as was the surreal sex toy and all his bindings. He slid down the side of the bar, only it wasn't a bar at all now. It was a tree. A tree in a quiet glade in the forest, the place he used to go when he was a boy. He'd buried a box of treasures in the roots, tangible things that could never be taken away, unlike hopes and dreams. Those types of illusions had been taken away from him by masters at dream stealing. He'd learned well, becoming exactly like them. *Do unto me and I shall do unto you, unto everyone that crosses my path.* If he dug into that box, would he find the dreams he had stolen from Narcissa, Lady Jane and the others? At the lifting of that lid, would those dreams fly away like souls, back to their Mistresses?

He tore away the grass covering and dug his fingers into the earth, the dirt pushing under his nails. Grunting at the exertion, he clawed deeper, flinging aside the handfuls of soil he dislodged.

It wasn't there. If he dug to China, he knew it still wouldn't be there. When he felt Dona put her hand on his back, the sobs rose up as hard and fast as the orgasm. He didn't cry. He was a man and men didn't cry. He turned, pressing his forehead into her legs, not daring to wrap his arms around her as he wanted to do. Dona had shaken everything loose with the pain and pleasure and he had nothing but despair now, despair at what he was.

For so long, the only emotions he'd shown to others had been calculated. The faces necessary to get what he thought he wanted. Now he knew why dolls were so often hollow molds. Nothing of substance inside.

At this moment, he thought he'd never wanted anything more than to belong, to be loved by a woman like her, but he had become something so far from that he had no hope left for being anything of worth at all.

Dona knew she didn't want to hear his raw thoughts. She'd had her heart shattered once before by a man. Her response at that time had been to pick up the shards and stab him with them. She knew everything Jonathan had done and the road and choices that had brought Nathan there. She knew the difference between repentance from cowardice and true remorse.

His soul was reaching out, groping for what he'd once thought he could be. The kid in the Superman cape standing on the street curb, imagining it was a building's edge, the world below depending on him to save it. Just as once she'd dreamed that she'd be the princess in the fairy tale, deserving of love, living happily ever after with the prince who would always adore her.

Or at least she and other lucky kids had believed in that. Nathan had had the dream snatched from him much earlier. Like her and the shards of her heart, he'd turned the dark landscape into the setting for nightmares to inflict upon others. While causality didn't absolve him, the soul of that little boy with the cape made her bend now, hold the shaking broad shoulders that were capable of shielding and offering a woman so much. Of being any woman's own private hero.

She was so much smaller than he was, Nathan had to wrap his arms around her legs after all to keep her upright when his sobs rocked them both, but she kept embracing him. Making soft crooning noises until it ebbed away, leaving him weary but too numb to sleep. He was in Hell, after all. Sleep wouldn't be possible here. No form of escape.

He'd never expected there to be a Heaven, so he realized Hell wasn't really all that surprising to him. Except Dona. Dona was the surprise. Tearing up his ass one moment, merciful the next, never letting him get away with anything, so

107

that in a remarkably short time she'd made him abandon the instincts of a lifetime. They were useless with her, leaving him only with himself. His horrible self.

"Where have you been? When I've been so lost…" He had to be babbling, because the words made no sense to his brain, but they felt right, coming from deep inside him. Some part of him wanted to keep repeating them, hold the words to him like a child's security blanket.

*Where were you? Why weren't you there to help save me from myself? Who are you?*

She touched the side of his face, her thumb caressing his lips. "You're not alone. We all get lost."

"I'm weak."

"No." She knelt before him now, an odd choice for a Mistress, for with his greater height it made him taller. But as she gently pressed him back on his haunches so they were knee to knee, she felt far larger than anything he could ever imagine being. She reached up, brushed his brow with her fingertips. "This isn't the forehead of a weak man. Not this strong jaw, or these wonderful eyes." She put both hands on either side of his neck. "You've made some terrible choices. But you're not weak."

"You don't know what it's like. You haven't fucked up the way I have."

She blinked, a harsh chuckle coming from her throat. "You want to know why I'm here? I'll show you, so you don't have any illusions."

The world began to swim around them, that sense of disorientation that was like being swept along in a vast ocean. He wished there was something to hold on to, but when he reached out, his hands met nothingness.

\* \* \* \* \*

He and Dona sat in an empty theater. The stage was the only illuminated area. He couldn't see aisles or walls, as if their platform of chairs was suspended over an abyss. He was in a tuxedo. Apparently she could dress or undress him from moment to moment as easily as she could a paper doll, a highly unsettling comparison.

A glance to his left showed his Mistress in box seat finery, a copper-colored dress that glittered and flowed to her ankles. Wearing an amber choker on her throat and matching teardrop earrings, she complemented him as if they were a well-to-do couple out for an evening of upscale entertainment. He wanted to reach out and touch her, but it felt as if there were a thin but impenetrable field between them, forcing him to keep his hands to himself.

"Watch," she whispered. The lights of the stage and the movement of her mouth showed a dusting of gold glitter on her cheeks. It was also on the slopes of her breasts, visible in the generous low cut of the dress.

He lingered on her face. Perhaps it was habit. A woman's face, her eyes and her body all held clues to her emotions. Once he'd been a master at translating that mysterious feminine language. He was probably the only man in the world who could comfortably translate all the meanings of the word "fine" when it came from a woman's lips.

Therefore, he sensed her tension, at a level so high she was almost paralyzed with it. It made him want to touch her even more.

*You're not alone.* She'd said it to him, but did *she* know that? Had something so terrible brought her here that she thought nothing could match it, isolating her forever?

He thought he saw something else glitter at her eye, a copper-colored teardrop about to fall. Obeying a compulsion he didn't completely understand, he leaned forward, broke through that field and placed his lips over it, over the corner of her eye.

She stiffened. He'd surprised her again, so he didn't push it, didn't bring his hands into it. He just brushed her with his lips, letting that one tear moisten them, pressing his forehead against her temple, closing his eyes, absorbing her tense vibrations.

"You're not alone, either," he said.

Her jaw trembled. She nodded toward the stage.

"Watch, Nathan."

Reluctantly he turned his gaze there.

He found himself looking into a dining room. An attractive man sat there, holding the hand of his dinner companion, a beautiful redhead with pale skin. A great deal of it visible, since they were both naked, eating pizza on fine china, laughing. Obviously lovers enjoying a weekend of playful fun. As Nathan watched, the man rubbed a slice of the pizza across her breasts, smearing sauce and cheese there in a primitive display, bending his head to suck the food off her skin. She enjoyed it for a moment, her chin lifted. Then she pushed away. Standing up on the chair, she stepped onto the table, spread her legs and put her hands on her hips, making a stern face as he caressed her ankles, his hands moving up her calves. "That's a very bad boy, Alex. Isn't that what your wife would say?"

She went down on all fours, positioning her breasts before him, hanging them over his plate. "You clean every bit of that off with your mouth, or you'll get a very severe paddling." Her eyes darkened with lust, her voice dropping to a whisper. "Play the games with me you play with her."

"They're not games, Pamela." His voice got rougher, lower, his gaze rising to meet hers as he flicked his tongue over the sauce. "You're my Mistress... See? Your nipples just hardened. I'll teach you to love making me beg."

As they bantered, a shadow moved into the doorway. Watching. When that shadow stepped out into the light of the stage, Nathan saw Dona in slacks and blazer, a professional career woman with the look of someone returning home from a business trip. From the darkness around him came a rush of sound, an invisible audience oohing like a class of dramatic schoolchildren, knowing someone was going to be in very big trouble.

"Dona, stop."

He couldn't turn his head from observing the stage to look at her, couldn't move at all. The darkness in the theater was absolute. He wouldn't have been so sure she was still there, except that whenever she was absent, like when she'd gone to see "Him", it felt different. Almost like they were two magnets.

Magnets. His thought resounded in Dona's head as she watched him through the darkness. Like Lucifer had said. They couldn't help but believe in one another. The way he'd kissed her just now, when he'd never reached out to a woman without calculated intent. It made her want to crawl over the seat into his lap, be held in those strong arms. She could sleep there, cradled against him, his heartbeat steady beneath her ear.

The voices on the stage drew her attention away, making her remember why such musings were dangerous.

"Dona..." Alex displayed the expected deer-in-the-headlights look. His gaze darted between the two women. Pamela was frozen on the top of the table. "You're...home early."

"Earlier than you think." Dona's voice was high, thin, but Nathan heard the hint of steel in it that he'd recognized from the first moment when she ordered him into her car. He also felt her pain like a full cannon blast in the chest. Blowing everything to pieces, an agony of disintegration of everything she was or knew.

He knew what that felt like. He'd experienced it before he'd even had a solid sense of self to call his own. For the first time in his life he thought that maybe it had been easier to be shattered early, rather than like this, when enough time had passed to allow a person to spin dreams so strong that they became a part of her, like a vital organ or limb.

He was seeing too much. More than she had seen or felt in herself when what was happening on the stage had actually occurred. Dona didn't understand how this involuntary one-sided telepathy would help. If Nathan's soul was as poisoned as Lucifer thought, all He was doing was arming Jonathan, because by letting her see what her charge was feeling, it was stripping her emotionally, making her feel vulnerable. Why was Lucifer doing this?

"I've been here long enough to see you eat more of that pizza than you should. You know your cholesterol numbers aren't what they should be." The Dona on stage glanced at Pamela, who looked as if she wished to be anywhere else in the world. "I guess worrying about that was a waste of time, though, wasn't it? A person has to *have* a heart to get heart disease."

A titter of audience laughter. It was so obscene against the frozen paleness of Dona's features on stage and the wooden quality of her voice that Nathan felt nauseous. "Cut it out, Dona."

Suddenly, he was able to look toward his current Dona. See her silhouette. Her eyes met his, glittered in the darkness. "That's a very appropriate comment," she said.

Pamela screamed and his attention jerked back to the stage. Dona had taken two steps forward and wrapped one hand in Alex's shoulder-length hair to pull his head back. In a fluid motion, she shoved a kitchen knife into his left pectoral. When Pamela's knees went out from under her, she landed on the plates, breaking one. The wineglasses fell over, rolled to the floor and shattered, spreading wet burgundy across the table linen. As she scrambled backward, blood sprayed out from Alex's chest over her, over all of it.

"So, let's see…" Dona grunted, jerking on the knife as her husband convulsed in death throes, his hands batting ineffectively at her. "There it is. You do have one, don't you?

Lucky I'm a surgeon. Otherwise I wouldn't have known where to find such a small thing."

Nathan swallowed, unable to look away but wanting to do so with all his will when Dona pulled the man's heart out of his chest, severing the attached arteries as matter-of-factly as she would have cut strings of cheese to free one of those slices of pizza from the main pie. Her blood-spattered face was an indifferent mask, her blouse soaked with his life fluids. When she turned on her practical black heel and advanced on Pamela, her husband's lover fell off the table, trying to get away. Dona backed her into a corner where the woman remained on her knees, arms up to protect herself as she babbled, sobbed, her gaze latched on that terrible thing in Dona's blood-soaked fingers.

"It's a large house, Pamela. I've been here since last night, a ghost flitting from room to room, staying just outside your notice." Dona's face was pale as a departed spirit, her dark eyes like a vampire's. Flat, emotionless. It clicked in Nathan's head. She shut down when she was feeling too much. He suspected that would have figured into her ability to be a surgeon, a successful one, for the opulence of the home strongly suggested she'd been important in her field.

"For thirteen hours I've been watching the man who made an oath to me proclaim his love for another. Fuck her, share thoughts about me with her. You knew he was married, but you were more than willing to help him break that oath. My soul died, Pamela, watching the two of you." The Dona on stage cocked her head, considering the knife in her opposite hand. Pamela curled back into herself, arms clasped over her legs as she became a ball, rocking, keening hysterically.

"It's okay if they kill me for this," Dona continued in a reassuring tone. "Why would I want to live in a world where the person who promised to love me above all others...forever...would do something like this?"

As if sensing imminent danger, Pamela uncurled abruptly and made an attempt to scramble past her. Dona thwarted it easily, putting her foot in the middle of the woman's chest and slamming her back on her ass in the confining corner. Then she squatted, bringing herself eye to eye with the redhead and holding the tumescent mass of blood and muscle before her horrified face.

"I'm going to call the police, Pamela. But before I let them come rescue you, you're going to eat this. Every bite. If you vomit, you'll eat it again, until it stays down. Then we'll call. Okay?" Her lips drew back from her teeth in a smile that was a death threat. Pamela's wide eyes registered it. "You wanted his heart? You're going to have it, every faithless bite."

The theater dimmed, blessedly, but Nathan wished he could block his ears. For the next fifteen minutes he heard the sounds of Pamela pleading, gagging, choking, pleading more, then finally her broken whimpers as she obeyed Dona's will and did the unthinkable. The theater was completely dark when he heard the sound of a phone being dialed and Dona's voice.

"Yes. I've killed my husband and his pathetic whore is in shock. Please come right away to…"

The voice faded, Dona giving details as calmly as if she was prescribing blood pressure medicine to a patient.

When the stage lights rose, it was just a velvet curtain. The two of them sat in an empty theater.

Nathan turned his head, studied Dona's profile. She did not move. Her attention was on the stage, her dark hair elegant and upswept, her neck pale and almost fragile beneath the clasp of the amber necklace.

"You were known as the Scorned Wife," he said. "That case was…"

"Thirty years ago. I refused counsel, pled guilty and let them put me to death. I didn't care. I thought my soul had been eaten, the way that heart was eaten." Her gaze turned to him now, a deep well of things so frightening that neither he nor any man he knew would have been brave enough to meet her gaze. He looked down at her lap, at her clasped hands, the fingers twisted together in a knot. He heard her mocking chuckle.

"It wasn't."

The theater went dark again and Nathan could see nothing, only hear Dona's breath next to him, the sound of her voice drifting over his skin.

"I wish I could look back on that now and say I don't know who that Dona was. That I can't relate to her and don't know what possessed me. Every act you commit, you commit consciously, even if it's so unspeakable that you make yourself believe something else compelled you to do it. Those hours I spent in the house while they didn't know I was there... Touching their body heat on my mattress where he and I had loved one another, so many ways. Watching her rifle through my closet while I stood a foot away from her in the shadow of my dresses. Listening to her make fun of me with the information he'd given her about me, about our relationship. I knew it was insecurity, making fun of what you don't understand. The adulteress's guilt at taking what she knows is rightfully another woman's. I felt angry with her, of course. It was all about him, though. The way he looked at her, smiled when she made the jokes. But he never laughed, because he knew what was between us. He was indulging her ignorance because he loved her. Because he no longer loved me.

"I should have left the house the minute I knew. I couldn't. It was like..."

Nathan wanted to reach out and find her hand, even as his mind told him the desire had all the wisdom of reaching into a snake's burrow, groping blindly toward a possible strike. She continued after a long pause. "When you find out a lover is unfaithful, it's usually a snippet of information. Bits and pieces of things that come together like a puzzle. There are a lot of doubts. I think I stayed so there would be absolutely no doubt in my mind, no way he could lie and make me think what I knew was true wasn't. I had to rub my nose in every bit

Joey W. Hill

of it, so by the time I reached that moment I was like a starving dog given the smell of blood in a sheep pen. I had to make him hurt, had to strike them both, even knowing they'd never feel a tenth of the pain I was feeling. Death was the only thing I could do to him that seemed anywhere close."

Another moment of silence, then she spoke again. "I found out he served a more severe punishment here than I did. Do you know why his crime is considered worse in Hell?"

He licked dry lips and braved it. Reaching across the seat, he found her hand again. "No."

It surprised Dona that he wanted to touch her after seeing what had happened on the stage. In prison, male guards had been more frightened of her than any other prisoner. She felt no fear or revulsion from Nathan. Only sympathy. But he didn't know the answer to the question. She could feel him thinking about it and knew his heart wasn't clean enough to find the answer. It twisted a knife in her own, knowing the answer was beyond his grasp.

"Because the soul can't die. A soul can become twisted, deformed, maimed, wounded, but it won't die. Wounds allow infection. You become an instrument of anger, hate and bitterness. You become what attacked your soul in the first place."

"No."

"Yes." Now she held him when he would have drawn back. "You've seen it in the pleasure you took in the suffering of your Mistresses. They're one of your mirrors."

Nathan wanted to deny it, wanted to rail at her, but in this place it was absurd to lie to himself. He tried for a subject change instead.

"So this is part of your punishment? Serving as a Mistress of Redemption?"

"No. My sentence is done. I accepted the role of a Mistress of Redemption."

"Is your husband…still here?"

116

"No. He served his time. He wasn't vicious, just thoughtless. He's now back in another life, paying his karmic debt."

"So Hell and Redemption are separate."

In the quiet of the theater, after the horror of what he'd just seen and knowing that somehow it connected to knowledge of himself he did not want to have, he wanted to pretend they were somewhere on Earth, just sharing a philosophical discussion. Part of him hoped she would relent, at last answer some of his questions to help him get a grip on what was happening. He couldn't deny any longer that he was somewhere way the fuck gone from Dorothy's Kansas. Another part of him didn't want any explanations. He simply wanted to sit in this quiet place with her and not return to a place of nightmares or choices. Hold her in his lap until all the pain that pursued them both melted away and left only blessed stillness.

What if this had been Earth and he'd been on a date with her? Maybe they'd have gone back to her apartment, the apartment of a young medical student. Him a roofer with rough palms, palms she wanted to feel on her smooth skin. He would have pleased her long into the night, loved her, never given her reason to doubt him...

As Dona felt the thoughts, saw the images in his mind, it made her want to be there with him. Remember a time when she'd believed in such pure moments. She could imagine him moving between her thighs on the sagging secondhand mattress, the curtains fluttering with a hot summer breeze. Her fan was going at high speed because she couldn't afford to pay for air conditioning as well as her textbooks.

Sometimes dreams were far more special during the time when you were making them, rather than after you believed you'd achieved them.

Here, alternate realities were within a Mistress's grasp if she wanted to see how it would play out, to help her with her task at hand. She could take the opportunity to create that moment, enjoy it with him and then wipe it off the slate of his memory, keep it only on hers. But as she slid into his imaginings, a different way things could have turned out, she knew this had nothing to do with the task at hand and everything to do with her own desires...

\* \* \* \* \*

Summer breeze flitting through the curtains. Bed stripped down to just sheets and his body stretched over her, giving her the pleasure of running her palms up his strong arms, braced on either side of her. Across the broadness of his back, down to his hips. Lean, a roofer's spare body, muscled and more broad-shouldered than expected. When he bent to her, catching her lips in a kiss that was somewhat off center because of the rhythm of his body stroking into hers, everything was dusky, soft at the edges in the quiet room, the noises of the street outside blending with the radio inside.

"Dona." He murmured her name, sinking deeper. She arched, wanting all of him and more.

"Mine," she whispered back, biting his lips a little harder, feeling him swell inside her at the sensual punishment, the claim on him.

"Yours," he agreed. "Forever, Mistress. Yours to fuck...however, whenever..." Humor glinted through his gaze, but something darker too.

"Mine to love."

Something got still in his face. She saw the shadows. Before they could claim him, take him away from her, she cupped his jaw. "The way love is meant to be," she whispered. "The way you've never known. Trust me, Nathan. Save both our souls. Trust me."

Bending, he took hold of her breast in his mouth, suckled gently while she cupped the back of his head, encouraging him to let the tension in his arms ease until he was lying full upon her. Plowed deep in the fertile earth of her body, he nourished himself from her breast. She could feel the desire in him. The need. She wondered if he knew how much she needed to know he would surrender to her. She stroked his hair. "I wish this was our reality. I wish I'd gotten to you sooner."

*I wish I'd let you keep your hair.* She watched it spill over her fingers, those beautiful ash blond locks bleached by the sun.

He didn't lift his head, for of course he couldn't hear what she related from another plane. God, his mouth. His mouth alone was worth his weight in gold. He suckled, licked, squeezed her with his calloused hands, arousing her so she didn't have to think. Not at this moment. She tightened her legs on him and his hand slid down her thigh, cupped her buttock, lifted her as he rose up over her now, letting her feel his slow thrusts become more powerful.

"Not until I say so," she managed on a breath. His eyes gleamed.

"Not until I make you scream. And I will, Mistress."

She reared up, clasping his neck to put her mouth on his. Not urgent nips and tongue thrusts despite the spiraling need in her, but slow caresses with her lips. She kept her eyes open so she could smooth his brow, watch his eyes close as he couldn't face what was in hers.

*I love you.*

When he shuddered, she moved to his temple, feeling his arms band around her back. Pulling her all the way up, he took her to a sitting position straddling him. Burying his face in her breasts again, he impaled her hard on his cock, making her gasp. She wanted him to look at her, tried to get him to lift his head.

"I can't..." His voice was hoarse.

"You can. You can give it all to me. You're a treasure. My treasure."

She squeezed down on him tight, feeling her own body convulse, so close... God, he was so perfect. So damaged and yet so perfect. This was the time when he hadn't had so much polish, when he was still learning how to use his pain as a weapon. Ironically, he'd already committed the crime that would take him irrevocably down that path. She could feel the guilt rising in him as her love frightened his subconscious into a corner, made him face that crime. She couldn't let him turn away from that mirror. She couldn't turn away from it either. She had to let go of this reality.

*This isn't your time together. It's an illusion that never was. A fantasy.*

The dream melted away and she was looking at the man a decade later. She could see all the evil clinging to him, like oozing green mud from a swamp. She knew what he looked like under all of that. It was her job to know. That was why cleaning it off was going to tear her apart.

\* \* \* \* \*

"There are three layers," she said at last. Nathan let out a breath, knowing he'd gotten a temporary reprieve.

"Hell, Redemption, Purgatory. They're like three spokes of a wheel and the Hall of Souls is the hub." Her voice was soft, rich, distracting him with the vision of her mouth. "Once you go through Hell or Redemption, whichever is necessary, you choose your next life in the Hall of Souls and return to Earth to pay your karmic debt."

"So our world is Purgatory."

"Yes and no. The mortal plane is a place for souls to pay karmic debts, but it's also the place where reincarnated souls without karmic debts to pay continue their lessons toward enlightenment. It's also a place for new souls to start their journey. Having all three in the same place gives those with more spiritual knowledge the chance to help guide those with less. We all move toward spiritual peace together. Just at different paces."

"So, what's the difference between Hell and Redemption?"

She hesitated. For some reason that brief pause created a coldness in the pit of his belly. The conversation had started naturally enough. A way to put off the inevitable. A small blessing of time to hear her voice, feel the grip of her hand. As the silence stretched out between them, the pleasure slipped away, as did her hand.

"Hell is pain," she said at last. "Horrible pain at every emotional and physical level of who you are. It's punishment for conscious sin and it's purification to the very marrow. It's reserved for souls who are so corrupted that it's the most efficient option for them. The soul enters the mortal plane as a new soul, starting its journey again with no memory of what came before."

"That's bad?"

"It means you've gone to the beginning of the Monopoly board. All the lessons must be relearned, the paths re-walked. The destination of ultimate enlightenment, of peace and tranquility, is as far away as it can get. It's like... How would you like to have to do school all over again? Starting in kindergarten and go through it all? Bullies, humiliation, not fitting in, et cetera. Without the benefit of any hindsight to give you a leg up, the 'if I knew now what I knew then'?"

"It would suck." Many images came to his mind, very few of them pleasant. Visions of his Mistresses he could take, but he would *not* revisit high school. "It would suck," he repeated, vehemently.

"Redemption is the process of using a lesser level of pain to get to the whys without erasing the memory. Breaking the crust of evil off of the soul, so to speak, giving it a fighting chance to make up for past wrongs on its next incarnation."

"Like a dental cleaning. Go to Redemption every six months before Hell happens."

She could see his face, though she was denying him the same ability. His wry smile distracted her. He had a clever mind, a natural charm. She wondered if he realized how genuinely funny he could be. However, right now it was a defense mechanism. She could see the memories from his teens surging into his mind, his frantic attempts to pull a curtain over them before he experienced them fully. A moment before, she'd cursed Lucifer for making it possible for her to see this, but seeing the face he was trying so hard to avoid seeing helped her remember why she was here.

When his Mistress did not laugh, Nathan swallowed. His stomach felt as if it were rubbing against the jagged edges of his spine. "So I avoided Hell." He made another attempt. "I guess that was some kind of miracle."

With the theater dark, he couldn't see her reaction. Could see nothing but thoughts like a blurred landscape flashing by, his foot pressing down on a useless brake in a car headed for a cliff.

"In a manner of speaking, yes, I guess it is." Her answer sounded cautious.

"Dona, how did I..." He needed to shut up or change topic. Everything in him screamed that ignorance was bliss. He wished he could see her face. "When can you leave here?"

"I could have left a decade ago. I chose to stay."

"Why would anyone stay here?"

"Because here evil only wears one mask. I know to the nth degree how good or bad someone is. No dissembling, no way to hide behind façades."

"No chance of love or happiness."

"I had that chance. I'd rather not risk pain like that again."

"So you'll never leave here. I'll never... After I leave... Dona..." He reached out in the dark, didn't question how he knew perfectly where her face was to cup the delicate oval in both hands. "No. *No,*" he repeated. Leaning forward, he pressed his forehead to hers. He was amazed that she hadn't drawn away from him—not that he would have let her at this moment if he could prevent it—but...

God in heaven, why was this so important?

"Dona, who *are* you to me? All of your...assignments... They don't all feel like this about you, do they?"

He was as much as admitting she'd drawn something out of him no one had, but his curiosity now burned more fiercely than his fear of giving her an advantage. A long moment passed as he held her face like that. He could feel her staring at him in the pitch darkness. When she drew back, he reluctantly let her go, feeling her jaw slide along his fingers, her chin as she turned her face back to the stage. "We all go through things in our lives." There was a tremor in her voice, a raw reaction that made him wonder if he was going to regret asking the question. "Some things we handle right. Some things we handle wrong. Do you know what we're most afraid of?"

He shook his head. "No."

"That no one will understand us. Nothing means anything if your soul believes it will always be lonely. Alone. You know how you sometimes wake up in the deadest part of the night by yourself and wonder if this is what it's like to die, not able to take anyone with you for company, to give you courage? It can be overwhelming."

He'd done that in prison countless times, his body drenched in a cold sweat of fear. What was strange was remembering having the same type of panic attacks in his expensive townhouse. As if all the trappings he'd collected around him were silent, futile sentinels against his nightmares.

"I don't know why they do many of the things they do, but the Lord and Lady knew that. Knew that even belief in Them wouldn't be enough to give most of us enough strength to realize our full potential. So They made us in Their image. For every one of us, there's a soul mate out there. We may not meet him or her in every lifetime, but the connection between us is felt, even when our lives don't touch."

He knew what she was going to say. He should have been ready to scoff, but it was as simple a truth as if she was about to tell him an innocuous fact. *My eyes are blue, I'm six foot three and...*

"You're my soul mate. I'm yours, you're mine. That's why I asked to be your Mistress in Redemption." She said it flatly, giving him a hint of the roiling sea of emotions going on behind the tone. "We can't help but want to be together, protect each other." He thought he heard a faint smile in her voice, but it had the cold desolation of a ghost. "You should take that as a sign of hope. The soul is so pure in its love that no matter what wrong paths we take, it has the ability to guide us."

When she began to draw away from him, he reached out, clamped his hand down on her wrist, holding her. "If you never leave here... Am I worth redeeming but not loving?"

The lights returned on dim mode so he could see her face. She wore the corset again. In stunned shock, he saw she'd been crying. The Goth makeup was smeared and running, turning her face into a mask.

"I don't know, Nathan. Are you worth it? Do I deserve you?"

The question punched him in the gut. All the crimes he'd committed flashed through his head, bringing back his despair. He'd been accused of so many things, but no one had ever asked him to pass sentence on himself. Not like this, where there was no way out of the answer.

Even with her makeup messed up she was beautiful. Her sin had been that she'd loved someone so much it had compelled her to commit a horrible crime of passion. He didn't feel worthy of even touching her now, so he withdrew his hand, folded it in his lap. He was still in the tux and wished he could be naked again, her slave rather than a boy playing dress-up, pretending to be a man who deserved to sit by her side.

"No, I'm not worth it. But you are. You're worth everything."

The seconds ticked away as she regarded him in silence. He could tell nothing of her reaction from her streaked face.

"I know you're my soul mate," she said in that non-emotive tone. "When you touch me, when our eyes meet, I know it, but I'm not ready for it. I may never be ready to make myself that vulnerable again."

"You would if you could believe in me. If you could believe in yourself. You're worth loving, Dona. Don't give up on that. Any man... I'd..." He stumbled to a halt, not sure where he was going. For the first time in his life he didn't want to say the perfect thing. He wanted to say the honest thing. The truth was he didn't deserve her. If he was her soul mate, the person supposed to keep her from feeling that deep-in-the-dark desolate loneliness, she was screwed, because he wasn't worth the shit on her shoe.

"It's time to face the rest of your mirrors." She spoke at last. "Can you do it? Shatter them and face what's left?"

"I...I don't know."

Her expression shifted. His terrifying Mistress was back, and the look in her eyes turned his bowels to water.

"It's not a choice. It's time, whether you think you're ready or not."

# Chapter Eight

ဆာ

The next setting for his merry-go-round was, appropriately, a circular chamber, a place that looked as if it were designed for performing rituals. Everything of earth or stone, torches in sconces on the walls. Dozens of mirrors were embedded in the rock stratum so it was hard to separate Dona and the other features of the room from their reflections. The odd wall treatments were not as distracting as what lay in the center of the room, however.

"Look at her." Dona moved around a large block of stone, her fingertips touching the bare back of the woman bound and bent over it, her legs manacled to the floor. "Spread before you. Helpless. Deserving punishment. You may strike her until you draw blood, make her scream. She'll have to tolerate it until you stop, for there's no other choice. There is no loss of consciousness, no death. In the cycles that are considered time down here, eventually she'll be given a moment of no pain, her back smooth as if she'd never been struck. Then it begins anew."

"A pain that's reality and illusion both," he murmured. Like his Mistress's tears that had streaked her makeup. In the transition to this chamber, the evidence of that had been wiped away. While she was as perfect and intimidating as if the moment had never existed, he didn't doubt the reality of that moment as he'd doubted some of the others.

"It will continue until she hears the message that the pain delivers."

He was unable to look away as Dona traced the bumps of the woman's spine. He could imagine it as his own spine, her fingers caressing him a moment before she would strike with a whip. The thought of that sent a shiver through him, brought a tightening to an already overtaxed groin. His testicles had permanently drawn up in pre-ejaculation mode and he wasn't sure if they'd ever drop again. Even in the most frightening moments, he'd stayed aroused, as if the ability to fuck was a male's most basic proof that he was alive, capable of action and meaning. Dona's proximity had done nothing to discourage that constant state of need.

"What's the message?"

"That crime has punishment. This is the punishment. After that, the debt must be paid, three times. That's karma and one of the reasons for reincarnating."

The vulnerability she'd shown him was gone. She was dispassionate, almost cruel. He'd found a key to her in watching the stage play, though. The more she felt, the less she revealed in her face. She didn't want to be his soul mate, but she hadn't denied she felt something for him. She'd said she wasn't ready.

Even in the midst of this, not knowing what awaited him except the certainty that it would be awful, he felt the wonder of that realization. If soul mates were a real thing, then it meant Dona *was* his Mistress. Now, forever, this life or the next. Whether she wanted him or not. So they'd always feel this connection to one another.

He realized abruptly that he was grasping something. Dropping his gaze, he found a whip there, a metal-tipped cat-o'-nine with a six-foot reach, his knuckles white on the handle. He lifted his attention to the small of the woman's back, her naked buttocks and thighs. Her eyes were blindfolded, a gag in her mouth. Her nose was running, her body rising and falling with quick breaths, showing her nervousness and anticipation of pain, either because she'd been here before or she could hear Dona's words.

His Mistress completed her circle to stand behind him. Now that long-nailed hand *was* running up the smooth skin of his back. She had him back in jeans only, so she played with the waistband, dipping her fingers just beneath the snug fit, teasing the crease of his ass. "Pain administered the right way shatters mirrors, so we can peer into the darkness of our souls with no tricks and see who we really are. What makes us evil."

Nathan's gaze lifted as light caught the mirrors. The woman still lay before him trembling, her fingers clenched helplessly into fists and the manacles holding her taut on the stone tablet, but all around them the mirrors were rising from the walls. No longer embedded, they were suspended in the air and rotating on their axes. It seemed they moved together as well as individually, giving the impression the room was moving. Disorienting him.

Dona pressed her full breasts against his back, her hands on his hips steadying him as he lurched. When her hand reached under his arm and closed on his wrist holding the whip, he tensed.

"You've never struck a woman. I find that intriguing, considering how much you hate us. Would you be able to bring this whip down if it were me helpless as she is? My legs spread so you could whip my cunt, mark my back until there was only blood?"

"No... *No.* I don't...hate women."

"I know that." Her touch dropped, her palm stroking over him. "But we make you very angry. We frighten you."

She lifted up on her toes, whispered in his ear. "What you really want is to be the one lying on this altar, waiting for my lash. For me to bring you the pain, deliver it to you like a gift. Ah... You got harder the moment the words left my mouth." When she closed her hand over him as much as the pants allowed, he couldn't help moving forward, pressing against her hand. "You need to look into the other mirrors."

"I don't want to."

"Yes, you do. You've never known what it means, Mistress and slave, but you've wanted to, so much. You've made it about vengeance and denied yourself true submission.

That's what will help you find what you really want. Look into the other mirrors."

He kept his gaze stubbornly glued to the reflection of her face in that one mirror directly before them. "Whether you want a soul mate or not, tell me you care about me. I know I'm not goddamned imagining it."

He needed to know there was someone at his back, even if he didn't deserve to have her there. Even if the idea that someone could guard his back in Hell was laughable, like asking for a glass of ice water and expecting to quench the fire. But there it was. He didn't see any other way he was going to find the courage to do what she commanded.

"Yes," she said at last. "I care about you. Nathan." She said his name softly. It was as if she had kissed him, held her lips to his for that never-long-enough feeling of acknowledgement, completion. "But love isn't about seeing someone with blinders on, though we all wish it was. Nothing is easy about love. As your Mistresses found out. You made them dependent with your games and tore them down piece by piece."

He wasn't prepared when she reached down, seized his wrist and snapped it forward. The flogger struck the pale skin of the woman's ass and she jumped, whimpering.

Nathan wrenched his arm away, dropping the weapon, but Dona shoved him. Stumbling forward, he fell full across the bound woman, his hips and cock against her ass, his stomach and chest pressed into the contours of her back. The broad set of his shoulders sheltered her neck. Gargoyles of stone at each corner of the stone table came to life. Before he could yell or jerk back in startled horror, they'd seized his wrists in their jaws, stretched him out so his nose was pressed into the crown of the woman's head. Their teeth bore down on his skin with painful pressure.

They captured his ankles in a similar fashion and pulled them out to flank the outside of the woman's legs so his full weight lay upon her and his cock was even more aware of the creases of her most private areas. Though he could not see her eyes, tears ran from beneath her blindfold. Her quivering lips pressed hard against the gag, small muffled sounds escaping from behind it, the only thing she could do since the gag prevented her from screaming. She smelled of blood, sweat and sex, a potent combination to his cock.

"What do you want, Nathan?" Dona had picked up the whip and it flicked around her, reached out to sting his ankles. "Do you want this punishment? Will you take the lash for her?"

"I'll take it from you. I want it from you." He tried to sound unaffected, but noted the hoarseness of his own voice when Dona stepped forward to curl her hand around his now bare testicles, squeezed. "I don't know why you bother with the jeans if you're just going to keep taking them off me."

"Because I can't decide which way I like your ass better. In or out of them. So I'm enjoying both. My own little indulgence."

Indulgence was the right word for it. Nathan had a firm, perfect ass, one of the best Dona had ever seen. It was a testament to his ferocity and determination that he hadn't been raped in prison far more often. She wished the moment called for a paddle, because she would have liked to make those muscular cheeks turn red with her strokes, watch him get harder at the stimulus. His buttocks would clench as he rubbed his cock against the woman beneath him involuntarily until the stimulation from Dona's spanking and the woman's bare skin made him spill his seed on her. Dona could imagine the way his shoulders would flex, the trembling strain of his powerful thighs, the taut rebellion in his face as his Mistress nevertheless made him come at her command.

Then again, she liked watching him walk in jeans. The way he'd looked when she picked him up, the denim holding him with just the right snugness at his ass and groin, the long thighs. He had a confidence when he walked. That casual sexiness that said he was aware he was packing a cock that no sane woman would refuse, because he knew exactly how to use it.

*The true bad boy… Her bad boy.*

She stroked one of the cheeks, following the curve with her fingers, the tight line between his buttocks. When he relaxed at her touch, her pussy clutched at the evidence that he was making himself open to her.

"You'd be such a wonderful sub if you just let yourself."

His head shifted as much as he could move it. She saw one blue eye staring cautiously at one of the mirrors to see her better. "Maybe I just need the right Mistress. You said as much."

"The right Mistress who knows when you're bullshitting her with charm and when you're not. I think you're angling for a spanking."

He raised a brow, and that wryness passed through his expression again. "There's a difference between bullshit and teasing, Mistress. I submit to your judgment."

Dona felt her lips quirk despite herself. Nathan had a dry sense of humor that his Jonathan side had never displayed, so the evidence of it now both amused and pleased her. Progress.

When his Mistress gave him an arch look, Nathan thought she did that well, going from intense emotion and pain to flirtation in a blink. Used to extremes of pain, he had enough room in his brain despite his present circumstances to appreciate it. So he growled, lifting his hips when she reached between his legs and pricked his cock with those sharpened nails. With Dona's hands on him, her thighs brushing the back of his, he saw his body in the mirrors, stretched out over the captured woman's in a deceptively protective pose, self-sacrificing. He looked powerful, but here he was, helpless to the woman who circled them, whom he outweighed and towered over, but who dominated his vision and his mind as he strained to see her. As he watched her lift another whip, a simple quirt, he felt his cock harden to pre-orgasmic rigidity, knowing what was coming.

Dona's breath left her, the sound she'd made when she brought his lips to her cunt at the oasis. As if all her nerves had drawn up in excitement. Damn if his cock didn't leak at the sound of her arousal, even as his back flinched when the whip came down, a stinging blow.

She didn't stop with that one stroke. His confidence at looking in the mirrors increased, for all he saw was her, wielding the quirt as his cock throbbed against the firm ass beneath him, that aroused organ all too cognizant of the bound woman's pussy and anal passage so close, so accessible. However, it was the pussy and ass of the woman behind him that captivated his attention as she shifted to land the strikes. He wanted to kneel between her legs again and run his tongue over the slick material, seduce her into peeling it off, letting him plunge into the soft folds behind it. Grip her buttocks and squeeze, holding her to his mouth.

"You warmed up, sweet thing?" Dona straddled his bare thigh, rubbing her crotch slowly up and down the length. Bending down, she let her hair brush his warmly smarting bare ass as her lips touched his left buttock, nipped him. "You want to fuck her, tied up helpless beneath you? It's the only control you've got. I suggest you stick that big, hard cock into her now, because in about thirty seconds you're only going to know pain. Maybe the suck of her cunt on your hard dick will distract you."

He gritted his teeth and refused to move, though he could feel how it would take him in, her hot wetness. He was sure it was more of Dona's sorcery, how vividly he was imagining it.

"No?" Her voice softened, just a minute amount, but his sharpened senses caught it. He'd pleased her and that was worth anything. Had to be. "Faithful slave. Your choice, then."

She picked up the cat, tossed the quirt away. He'd never been struck by a metal-tipped flogger, but he knew the quirt would feel like a feather in comparison. He took a shallow breath, his hands starting to curl into fists. Then he stopped, made them relax. Let her see he would take her punishment. Welcome it. Pressing his face into the woman's hair, he heard her whimper as he set his teeth to a stranger's shoulder to keep from crying out.

The whip tore flesh on its very first strike. Dona brought it whistling down with strength on the length of his back, licking at his shoulder. It snagged, pulling skin and telling him the tips had been barbed. He was wrong. He hadn't anticipated this level of pain. Holy God, that hurt. Because the bindings held him so taut, he was denied even the minute relief of thrashing. The woman had gone rigid in fear and his cock was trapped in the channel between her buttocks, feeling the quivering clench of her ass.

He'd used a metal-tipped, barbed cat before. Not expertly. He'd flogged Detective Mac Nighthorse with one at the S&M Killer's behest. As he'd torn open the man's back, he'd rationalized that he was making superficial cuts, just a little more over the top than a flogging with more commonly used BDSM tools.

What the hell had he been thinking?

Another lash fell. Another. Pain was fire, sweat and blood beginning to burn across the field of his skin. The woman beneath him shuddered as he bit down, reacting to each strike.

Staccato flashes of thought strobed through his mind, adding to the agony. Was Dona right? Was he like the S&M Killer? Had he hated Nighthorse that much? Had there been a moment he'd *wanted* her to kill the cop? Maybe that's why he'd gotten five years when his attorney estimated three. The judge had sensed it in him, the potential. As the pain built into a roaring crescendo, drowning out everything else, he began to wonder. Maybe he *was* evil… He never thought of his very last Mistress by her given name because it brought back images of other things they'd shared. Things that hadn't been about death and mayhem…

*Stop it. That's bullshit.* But the pain drove everything but the most horrible possibilities from his mind.

Mac Nighthorse had not cried out, but then the murderess had told him up front it would be ten strikes. Mac hadn't been in some surreal dream of Hell where the strikes could conceivably fall forever, with the torment building and building, no oblivion promised or hoped for.

Still, Nathan took some grim satisfaction in the fact he held out past fifteen before he cried out, when Dona started crisscrossing the same open flesh. At thirty he was screaming, his hands clenched into hard fists as he pulled against his restraints with enough strength to dislocate his bones. The gargoyles were implacable, not giving even a millimeter of relief as it continued and continued. He stopped wanting. He just became a creation of pain, wanting to pass out, knowing he wouldn't.

*Please, Mistress. Have mercy...* How much torture could he bear for her pleasure? To win her gentlest touch, the kiss of her lips...

"Look at the mirrors." Dona was suddenly at his head, grabbing his chin and jerking it up, making him look. He blinked through tears, tasting the blood of his bitten tongue. The shadows were back, just as he knew they would be, flirting at the edges. Oh God, his back and ass were in agony, his shoulders. He was almost grateful not to see images of himself, because he didn't think he could handle seeing his back stripped of skin. Whatever was left had to be hanging off the altar in gruesome ribbons. He hurt so much he wanted to throw up, loose his bowels, but he knew that wouldn't happen. The inability of his body to function as it naturally would under extreme duress underscored how long she could keep doing this—forever if she wanted to do so.

The mirrors swam with colors and Mistress Lauren materialized in the mirror directly in front of him. Quietly serene and so temptingly strong. Hair like golden wheat and eyes like the summer sky, just like the books said. The one that hadn't been in the dance crowd, because she was different, just as Dona said.

"The others you decimated in three or four months. You probably could have done it sooner, if you didn't enjoy taunting and playing with your prey so much. With Lauren, you had to play the game a hundred percent for almost a year. Couldn't jerk her chain the way you did with so many others, running hot and cold from day to day, playing with their baggage. First time you tried, she almost left you. So you realized to win this round you'd have to be the perfect sub in all ways. No gratifying little torments."

"No... It wasn't like that." His voice was hoarse, the words clumsy with his tongue bitten and swollen. She pressed on, ignoring him.

"When you'd completely won her trust, you'd break it off. Because you couldn't play with her until that point, the only way to let her know what you'd done was to do it with just the right expression. A little smirk, an offhand attitude. I bet you practiced that look in the mirror for days. It had to be clear as a stop sign. In one blink, she'd understand that the past twelve months of her life, the vulnerabilities and love she'd offered you, had meant less than nothing. Making her feel like she was less than nothing."

The moment was there, all around them. The night Lauren had told him she wanted more with him. Wanted it all. The transformation as his rejection registered. Her disbelief, the incredible shock.

When Nathan looked at Lauren's face, he saw what he hadn't seen then in the glow of his triumph. A stricken desolation in her expression that made the beating he'd just taken look like a toe-stubbing. He had stabbed her through her soul.

*No. That's absurd, the fucking manipulation of this place. She was fine. I wanted...*

"You didn't know what you wanted by that time, Jonathan. Just like an addict, the getting became everything.

The worse your soul felt, the more you craved to do it. That's why the next Mistress you chose turned out to be a psychopathic serial killer."

"I don't know what you're talking about," he said hoarsely. He just wanted those images to go away. He'd seen it. *Fine. Take it away.*

"Shut up," Dona said mildly. The cat twitched in her hand, making him flinch. If she struck him again, he was pretty sure she'd strip exposed muscle, leave grooves in his organs. "The soul can take only so much bullshit before it seeks annihilation, even if the rational mind isn't aware that it's being tugged into harm's way. The soul is the catastrophe center. Too many people, too much strain on the environment, here comes a tornado or an earthquake, not only to reduce numbers, but to remind us there are consequences, things bigger than ourselves. If we create imbalance, it will be balanced. The S&M Killer was your tornado, so you thought she destroyed your life. But it was Lauren that made you step into her path."

The shadows took Lauren away, but the mirrors were moving, closing in on him like the inside of a funhouse. Dona was behind him again, increasing his apprehension.

"Is this Hell's pathetic copycat version of Dickens?" He said it through clenched teeth. Fighting panic. He could hear his heart beating irregularly, responding to the stress of the pain even if it could not succumb to it. His fluids made him stick wetly to the faceless, nameless woman beneath him. He wanted her gone too. He wanted it all gone.

Dona chuckled, the sound grating on his nerves at the evidence that he could not shake her, even as his body responded traitorously to the sultry tones of her voice.

"Do you know why you hated Mac? So much that it clouded your judgment and landed you in prison?"

"Because he was a cop, and bullshit."

She lifted a brow. "Because he got what you've always wanted."

"I didn't want Violet. But I could have taken her away from him if I wanted to do it."

"Mac Nighthorse would have ripped your arms off if you'd so much as breathed on her. You know I'm not talking about Violet. Don't fuck with me. Don't fuck with yourself."

The mirrors turned and now Dona was holding a bullwhip with the diameter of a python. *No. Please...* He swallowed, bit back the plea. The fact she was holding a new whip meant she'd be using it.

"What is it Mac had that you want? What is it that Lauren found after you mercifully left her life?"

He shook his head. A moment later his body arched, a scream tearing the lining from his throat as the bullwhip landed a full stripe down his back that made his upper body feel as if it had been seared by acid. His muscles constricted against the pain so forcefully he thought he felt his ribs crack under the strain. His head snapped down, inadvertently striking the temple of his bound companion. She made a sound of pain.

"*Trust.* Trust in a Mistress." Dona answered the question. "Nirvana with a Mistress. The ability to let go and believe she'll take care of you. The state where bringing her pleasure becomes the most important thing in your life."

Four more lashes, one for each point. He'd never thought there could be such a level of pain. The whip snagged the strips of skin that remained, ripping them loose. More blood ran down his sides, making him itch. The chamber echoed his cries, overlapping, bouncing back on him, making his head scream with agony.

"You thought Mac could see that weakness in you, the fact you didn't have what it took to get there with a woman." Her voice penetrated all of it. "When we're insecure, we make up stories of what people see when they look at us. Funhouse mirrors again, mocking us so that we project the images of others over the image of ourselves. But it always comes back to you, because that's the only thing any of us control in this life. You made the choices that put you here."

With the bones of his wrists grinding against the stone hold of the gargoyles, he couldn't control the spasmodic convulsions of his upper body as he waited for the next blow to come. He could barely open his eyes, clogged with tears and perspiration running off his brow. He was as cold as he imagined death felt, and would have welcomed it if that was what it heralded.

Two minutes of silence passed, punctuated only by his rattling breath and the woman's frightened noises beneath him. Saliva from his clenched teeth had dampened her hair.

Lifting his lashes, he looked for Dona in the mirrors. He blinked, trying to wet his parched lips with his abused tongue. Trying to focus, because he wasn't sure if what he was seeing was real.

The mirrors showed an image from the past, a few moments ago. Dona whipping him. She was crying, a sob breaking from her lips at his every scream.

Then it was gone as if it had never been and those shadows were moving again. Was the quick glimpse reality or illusion? It didn't matter. Her tears for him caused a different kind of anguish, one that striped him from the inside, lashed his vital organs in truth. Breaking him down in a way even the extremes of physical pain could not.

As she circled the tablet now, he didn't see any evidence of her distress on her face, but he knew now that reality here changed every moment. He stiffened as she touched his back, but she was touching smooth skin, skin that no longer felt the pain, though the experience was indelibly printed on his mind. His limbs were still trembling from the lingering effects. The tears, discharge from his nose and saliva from the corners of his mouth remaining from the torture made him avoid focusing on his own image.

Dona bent before him, her hair tumbling over her shoulders. He was ashamed for her to see him like this. When he tried to duck his head, she merely caught his chin, lifted it and began to wipe him clean with a soft handkerchief.

"Vain man. Always so vain. Be still."

He swallowed, his eyes falling shut. He'd survived her lash, but he didn't think he could survive her tenderness. He was going to break into a million pieces, just like a mirror, cursing himself seven years times forever. Or perhaps that deed was already well and done.

When she dabbed at his eyes, her voice was soft but merciless as the lash. "Mistress Lauren would have loved you, kept you, but you couldn't stand that. You had to use her, make her fall in love with you. You had to tell her in every way she'd been a fool, that you'd played with her mind from the first. She's one of the mirrors. Look into her eyes and see yourself. I wonder what you would say to her if you could see her now, at this very moment?"

\* \* \* \* \*

He was in a park, standing at the entrance to a small private glade where a woman sat on a picnic blanket. Her lover was stretched out there as she pushed up his T-shirt, ran an ice cube slowly down his flat, hard stomach, traced the curve of his navel as he trembled. His lean arms, marked with Celtic-styled tattoos, were curved behind his head, the self-restraint at her behest, Nathan was sure. When the woman turned her head, she saw Nathan.

It was Lauren. Her blue eyes freezing, she stood, the ice dropping from her fingers. Her lover rose beside her, a man with gray intent eyes that shifted between the two of them, taking the situation in at a glance. His expression told Nathan that he knew his history with his Mistress. He underscored that by stepping up to her side. No, even somewhat in front of her, an unmistakably protective motion.

He had tried to love Lauren. In the end, it was safer to believe she was like all the others. Looking at her now, he saw the inner and outer beauty that had always been there. The pure strength of the love she'd given to this man next to her, binding him to her. The face of her lover reciprocated that devotion in spades. He wouldn't hurt her like Nathan had.

"I never deserved you," he said hoarsely. "I betrayed you, and all you ever offered me was love. I'm sorry."

He wasn't even sure where the words came from. It was as if the pain Dona had been inflicting on him since he'd come into her care had opened a well inside him that was filled with simple truth. All it took was dipping a bucket into it to offer it to himself. To Lauren.

Dona's whip snaked through the air, struck. The park, Lauren and her lover exploded in a shower of glass, the mirror shattering outward. He would have ducked his head, but in the air the shards became silver confetti, glittering as they settled on the floor, on Dona's hair, across the ample tops of her breasts.

In the shards still floating through the air he saw the image of the corpulent woman again. *Such a pretty little boy...*

# Chapter Nine

## ⊗

He closed his eyes. As he did, he became cognizant of the woman beneath him, still trembling. He felt an odd urge to stroke her hair, soothe her. Almost as he had the thought, his hand was free, so he did it tentatively, though the rest of his body remained bound so that all he could do was stroke her hair with the one hand. Moving to the side of her face, he followed the tracks of the tears coming from beneath the blindfold. When he touched her lips stretched around the ball gag, they quivered, but she didn't make any other movement.

"She endures this every day?"

"Yes." Dona stepped over his legs, stood behind him. Daring a gaze into the mirror again, he was relieved to see them in present time. Leaning forward, she propped her elbows on the small of his back, those generous breasts shaped into tempting globes over the edge of the corset. Her pelvis brushed the base of his buttocks, her thighs teasing his testicles.

"I'm going to use your cock now. Because it's my cock to do with as I please. You'll move only at my direction, as if it's attached to me in truth. You're going to be my strap-on."

She straightened, unclipped the belt triple-looped low on her hips, the one that was decorated gypsy fashion with tiny sun discs and moon crescents done in beaten metal that made a sultry chime sound as she moved. It did so now as she removed it, reached under him and double-looped it around his cock and balls. Bringing the remaining ends of the belt up past his hips and around hers, she re-latched it at the flare of her buttocks. The rotating mirrors gave him the ability to see them at all angles. Now she was pressed to his ass, her thighs

in tight and straight between his spread ones. Putting her
hands on his hips, she lifted her own, drawing him back with
her, moving up, then down, pressing him against the ass of the
woman whose lips had tightened, in fear or anticipation he did
not know. The blindfold slipped so he could see her eyes, wide
and frightened, bright blue like Lauren's, blonde hair spilling
over her shoulders as the gargoyles pulled the blindfold
completely away and re-secured his hand.

"No."

"You have no right to say no. You're my strap-on cock
and you'll do exactly as that mindless, hungering dick of yours
would do."

"She's looking at me. She's afraid."

"You had no compunction about fucking Lauren over,
figuratively. Now shut up. You're hard as a rock."

He was. It seemed he had been erect nonstop since he got
into Dona's car. It made no sense, except that he'd been filled
with an undeniable hunger since she came over that hill. As if
sinking into her body might heal so many of the things inside
him that were as raw and exposed as his back had been under
her lash. What was beneath his cock was incidental. His
arousal was centered on what was behind him. Dona's thighs,
her breath on his bare back, her fingers digging into his hips,
moving him exactly as she wanted to move him, the way a
man would fuck a woman. She even gave a guttural sound of
satisfaction as she made the right adjustment and he sank deep
into the woman's accessible pussy. She writhed, whimpering
around her gag, but he felt how wet she was. The fear in her
eyes was mixed with self-loathing.

"She can't help but enjoy your big cock. What woman
wouldn't?"

The woman's eyes changed, became trusting, too
innocent, too blue, reminding him of other, even more painful
memories. He tried to fight against Dona. He should have been

strong enough to overpower her, but not with his arms and legs bound.

His cock wanted to thrust more eagerly, but he wanted to pull his body away from the woman he was being forced to rut upon. The jagged edges of the sunbursts and points of the crescent moon jabbed into him, goading his cock like spurs as Dona rocked him forward, thrust, withdrew. He tried a different strategy, deepening the power of his thrusts to increase the speed and get it done with, but she used the belt like reins, drawing them taut, embedding those points more deeply. Cursing, he was forced to stay at her pace while she laughed at him, a taunting, velvet caress in his ears, reminding him she had all the power, all the control.

She had to know it wasn't this nameless woman's cunt drawing him closer to orgasm. It was the way Dona was controlling him, teasing him, the images that rose in his own mind called by no one but himself. Of her sliding on an actual strap-on with a clitoral stimulator, fucking him the way a Mistress gave herself the privilege to do, driving herself to climax while her slave suffered jetting into a condom. But there had to be that blessed moment when she'd straddle him, sink down on his cock while he trembled, obeying her will for the better-than-dying pleasure of watching her rise and fall on him, letting him serve her.

"That's it, baby." He heard the lust and demand in her voice, rippling over him like the rake of her nails. "You're such a good cock for your Mistress. Are you going to come for me?"

He groaned in answer, his head bending down. She yanked, drawing the chains cruelly into him, sending pain rocketing through his groin.

"As Mistress demands."

"You're just playing with me. Charming me, fucking with my mind like all those other women." She drew harder on the belt and yet this time drove him forward so the decorative metal disks pierced his cock, the agony roaring through his mind so he could barely speak, only beg.

"No...Mistress Dona...please..."

"Feel this." Her fingers came between them, penetrated his ass, burying deep.

He climaxed in an instant, a burning pleasure and pain like having his guts wrenched out by the denizens of Hell while being treated to the pure light of Heaven.

He screamed, jerking, pumping on his own, Dona's hands allowing him to drive into the girl at his own pace now, as brutal and mindless as a stallion. She cried out around her gag, her cunt convulsing, a tight orgasm that spurred his, especially with Dona's hand deep within him, fisting him now, driving up the pain quotient so that he knew this had to be an otherworldly realm. No man could climax while under such torture that broke down his mind. It was the true essence of Hell. Finding the heights of pleasure a man sought his whole life, but experiencing it only at the price of a pain that would turn his bowels to water.

He could bear no more. "Please, Mistress...mercy..." He didn't know how his cock could be attached to his body still. More sweat or blood or both had to be running down his legs. As if she sensed his thoughts, his tormentor withdrew her hand, making him groan. She thrust her other hand between his legs, closed it around his wet, sticky member at the base, her fingers erotically caressing the joining point between his buried cock and the girl's stretched pussy.

Dona straightened then, her hand pulling back. She released the belt from her waist, but looped it around and tightened it on him like the cinch strap on a bull's testicles, only he didn't have the ability to buck to try to relieve the torturous pain. When she came around the table, she let him see her hand, wet with blood and his cum. Turning away, she curved backward toward him in a lithe move worthy of a circus performer. His cock suddenly was exposed to the air as his partner in torment vanished. He was bound alone on the altar and the gargoyles lifted their heads, drawing his upper torso a foot above the altar to allow Dona to arch along the table's edge just below his mouth.

He could not imagine how tightly she was laced in that corset to prevent her breasts from coming out of the garment, but the nipples remained out of view. Just.

Taking her hand, she brushed the blood and semen across the tops of those straining breasts as if painting a canvas, her fingers artfully marking her skin.

"Your seed, your blood, your sweat." Her dark eyes burned into his. "Lick it off me. When every bit of it is gone, I'll free your cock."

In the life that seemed a century ago, he would have turned on charm and his not inconsiderable sex appeal to get his way, but the Mistress who'd insinuated her upper torso under his mouth had outmaneuvered him at every turn. He was in too much pain now to take the risk. She was not a Mistress of Mercy, or one who let the needs of her cunt or heart drive her. For some reason, knowing the latter bothered him personally, not competitively.

It was his total submission she craved and demanded, no matter his pain. He understood that. The wonder of it was, though his cock screamed for release from its torture, saliva pooled in his mouth at the anticipated privilege of touching his mouth to her skin.

Loosening the top lacing of the corset, she arched her back further. Her breasts spilled completely free, nipples pink, that incredibly delicate female color. Earlier, when she first fucked him, he'd expected them to be rouged black or dark red, like her makeup. The feminine contrast fascinated him.

Catching his chin with one hand as the gargoyles started to bring him within touching distance, she dug in her nails to command his attention. "Don't touch my nipples with your mouth. Not until I permit it. Now get busy. I want your filth off of me."

She had said his mouth couldn't touch her nipples, but she'd said nothing about how often his forehead or the coarse silk of his eyebrows could caress those beautiful plump tips. He strained forward, laid his open mouth over the top of one curve and began to lick. Suck, nip, taste her skin, tease her, reveling in the ability to at last touch her. For a few moments that was all that was in his mind. That, and the torture going on in his groin area. He followed her command to the letter so he could have this sensation, even while his genitals felt like they were in the clamp of a bear trap. He pleasured her, not for any calculated reason or to persuade her to release him sooner. That was up to her. He just had to please her. She'd release him if he did a good job, obeyed her Will fully. That was all his lust let him think about.

God, he would have been willing to stay in the torture device in which she'd encased his cock another eternity for the right to suckle that sweet nipple that was hardening against his temple. Her lips pressed against the base of his neck and he wanted to dip his head, kiss her mouth. But the way she was arched up against his mouth now, he knew what she wanted most.

"Please, Mistress. Let me suck on you. Please." He murmured it against her skin, felt her touch his bare scalp, stroking him. He saw a spot of blood on the side of her neck, just a fleck. She'd said every bit, hadn't she?

Her breath drew in as he reached it. Her fingers tightened. The triumph he felt sent a surge of blood into his cock that nearly caused him to cry out in agony. For once the satisfaction he felt at a woman's response was not the satisfaction of a predator, but of a man coaxing a reaction out of a woman he desired, a lover, a Mistress he wanted to please, to serve. He liked the feeling. Liked it enough to keep nibbling on her throat, despite the tearing fire in his groin and the bite of those metal discs.

Her hand curved over the back of his head, caressing the base of his skull. He wondered that anyone would think that

146

heaven was north when dealing with Dona's well-built body. When she guided his mouth over her right nipple, her voice was the answer to a prayer.

"Suck on me."

As he fastened on her eagerly, the reality changed, the pain and restraint on his groin area gone. They were no longer at the tablet that had reminded him uneasily of a sacrificial altar. The mirrors turned, showing Dona stretched out on a luxurious fainting couch, tossed with velvet throws. One of her knees was bent, allowing her leg to lean against the side of the back cushion so her legs in the tight pants were spread wide, taunting his peripheral vision with the lazy rock of that knee. The fabric at her crotch creased with the back-and-forth movement as he knelt on the floor next to her, his head beneath her hand. His hands were bound behind his back as he nursed her eagerly, wishing he could palm the full roundness of the breast in his two hands. She had such large nipples, like the sweetest of pale pink marshmallows, gone firm as gumdrops beneath his tongue and lips.

He was skilled at pleasing a woman and yet he'd never done it as he did it now, to prove to her that he was worth having at her side...

Daring to look up, he saw her lips were parted, color flushed. Her breath whispered from her in an excited cadence. He wanted his hands free, wanted to have her permission to touch those slick, soft lips between her legs, the globes of her buttocks so well defined but not revealed. If he could, he could make her writhe. Feel her softness... Make her lose control... Taste those gumdrop nipples... She'd be his then, and he'd have the upper hand... He could make her beg. Even in Hell he could win.

*Do you want your candy now?*

He jerked back, his head rising at the insidious whisper, the taste of gumdrops on his tongue. The mirrors turned and a shadow became that hated image again, a woman of enormous size, three hundred pounds encased in tight stretch pedal pushers and a sweatshirt with the Disney Siamese cats from *Lady and the Tramp* on it. She held out a handful of candy in her hand. She had nails as long as steak knives, as they'd been in his childish memory.

Stumbling away from the couch, he spat, trying to get rid of the sickly sugar taste. He told himself if he'd been close enough he would have tried to hit Dona with the spittle. He would have dared it, no matter the consequences.

"So did you taste like that on purpose?" He made it an accusation, but the anger was already slipping away. His heart wasn't in it. He'd been so close to something...different. Hadn't he? She'd duped him.

"No. That was you, Jonathan. Your desire to manipulate me was about to rise, driving away your joy in the simple act of pleasing me. This is another of your mirrors, called at your behest. Pity, because you were pleasing me quite well."

Dona rose, every hair and item of clothing in place, and drew his attention to the turning mirrors. "Foster mother number one..." she observed, touching the glass. The image rippled as if it were water she had disturbed. Pieces of the woman were picked up on all the mirrors around them. A profile, a close-up of her ear, her mouth, a fat thigh, a meaty hand, all flashing at him, making him feel sick, disoriented. "She thought you ate too much."

"She fucking tried to starve me." The words scraped in his throat. "When I tried to steal food from the kitchen, she caught me at it. After that, she'd throw my food in the backyard, make me eat it on my hands and knees like I was a dog. It was a rural area, no close neighbors. Sometimes she'd chain me out there with a collar, tell me if I took it off I wouldn't get any dinner at all."

He stood upright, alone. Sweating, trembling, facing that image. As the mirrors kept turning, moving, he lost sight of Dona. Anger rose up in him at that hated face, all the horrible, disgusting features. Dona had known what she was doing, slashing him open with Lauren and then pouring his worst foster mother like salt into that wound. But she wouldn't defeat him. None of them would.

"So I learned. Learned what drove her. She was going to throw some candy out in the yard one day, one measly piece for me when she had a whole box. I told her I wanted to eat it out of her lap, like a good dog would. Eat only from the hand of his Mistress. You should have seen the light that rose in her eyes." His lip curled up in an almost canine snarl, remembering how it quickly became a daily routine.

*"Little boys are just hound dogs." She nodded, studying him with green eyes the color of institutional walls. "Your dinner's buried in the backyard. Go find it, eat every bite and come back to get dessert." She opened her pants, dropped the candy down and wiggled until it became a lumpy expanse at her crotch. "You'll get your dessert then. Teach you to waste food and sass me. Chain you up in the yard if you don't behave."*

It disgusted him, not just because it was a horrible memory, but because he'd figured out the solution by twisting a compulsion he'd had, even so young. There was something beckoning to him, a desire to serve a woman, be her slave, but in an entirely different way… He'd used it to defend himself. Just as Dona used her undeniable need to be a Mistress to serve the purposes of Redemption, he'd used his undeniable craving to be a submissive to make it through the foster care system.

*You had to twist a gift a woman should treasure into a hideous weapon. It helped destroy your soul, your faith in women entirely. You were an innocent then. You can't blame yourself for that one. You were a survivor, Nathan, and you used the only tool you had. Instinct.*

He wasn't an innocent victim. Things had happened later…

*At that point you* were *innocent. The rest happened later.*

He shook his head, shook the words away from him as if he were scattering the shards of the mirror Dona had broken earlier. "It clicked then. Every woman had a weak side, a darkness. I just had to figure out her light switch, turn her on and off, and then I could have anything I wanted from her." He glared defiantly at that image. "I ate good after that. She let me sleep on the floor by her bed, instead of out in the yard. Until social services found out about her and moved me on again."

Before prison, he'd considered himself fit. He'd taken martial arts, self-defense courses, had owned and known how to use a gun on a practice range. Once in prison, he'd realized he knew nothing about the level of fitness required for survival versus show. But adaptability had gotten him through the foster care system, drove him to learn about table manners and dressing well so he could appear like a well-to-do stockbroker who had never experienced anything but private schools and church on Sunday. That adaptability had allowed him to change again. Suffering through the beatings, what passed for "routine" rape and a couple of serious gang rapes, he'd found out how to turn fitness into dangerous strength and agility, both of mind and body.

Which was why now he didn't hesitate to take two strides forward and plunge his fist into the glass, shattering his foster mother's face. The glass cut but the blood flowed out clean from his knuckles, a purification. The shattered pieces were there for one satisfying moment. Then they were gone, the mirror remade around his plunged fist. Sucking him in, it seized his other wrist when he punched at it to make it let him go. Now he was held fast. The shadows in the mirror shifted like the face of a Grim Reaper in the cowl of His robe, elusive but dreadful.

"Dona…" He despised himself for the panic in his voice, but those shadows were coming closer and he knew what had to be behind them. "Dona!"

"I'm here." Her hands, cool and almost gentle in their ruthless implacability, closed on his waist. Though he couldn't turn and see her, she was naked. Her bare breasts mashed lightly against his skin. The length of her smooth thigh was soft against his. Her pubic mound brushed the seam of his buttocks. Just a beautiful woman, simple and pure against his own nakedness.

"It won't let me go."

"I know. You want to break the mirror, but you won't let go of what created it. You're holding yourself."

"There are more..."

"Six foster mothers. The last one who had you took in ten children and only had time to make sure you were dressed and sent off to school each day. That was probably the best of the lot."

The shadows started to form images. "No." He jerked, but the glass held fast. Dona's arms circled his waist, her fingers playing absently along the top of his cock. Now he was face-to-face with the obscenely layered images of all of them. There was a reason six was considered an evil number. Violence, apathy, gluttony, indifference, greed and perversity. Six creative ways to rip away the outer shell of a child and thrust a man out of the remains, leaving him shivering and unformed to face the world.

He had to calm down. Dona's hands were devastatingly tender. Somehow that made it both better and worse.

"They destroyed the perfect human being you would have become. That's what you think, don't you? In the deepest part of your heart, the only place you don't lie to yourself, you think you're garbage because you came from garbage. Because you were abandoned like garbage."

"Please, stop." He hated begging. Not the mocking kind he did to win a Mistress's favor, not even the kind he'd done in reaction to his physical passion for her, but the true, bottom-of-his-gut pleading for something to take away the pain, the hurt. That kind of begging was an admission that someone had been able to hurt him, that he would have to rely on someone else. He hated it. Hated anyone who made him feel it, except he seemed incapable of hating Dona. He just wanted her to stop. "Don't do this."

"Sshhh. Look."

He'd rather have been boiled alive. He looked at the new image, his foster mothers gone as if they'd never been, except they were imprinted on his own life in ways it was getting hard to deny.

This woman was younger than he'd remembered her. She wasn't more than nineteen. Limp blonde hair, the sunken cheeks of an addict, hopeless blue eyes the color of his own. She'd taken him to a homeless shelter, told him to stay there. Not even that she'd be back. Just, "stay here". In about an hour one of the men who stayed in the shelter had noticed him, taken him to the priest, who in turn called the police and social services. The cogs of the machine began to turn, to grind him up. He could still remember the confusion, the desperation of having no control. Of wishing, forever it seemed, that she would come back and give him the chance to be better.

"Your mother." Dona's voice, quiet. When her hands moved to his arms, rubbing them even as they were held fast, he couldn't push away the memory or keep himself from saying it.

"I sat on her lap once. Tracing the needle tracks on her arms. She took a pen and helped me connect them to draw animal shapes. It was a game and she smiled at me... We made an elephant, sort of. She hugged me. She got high later that night, threw a beer bottle at me to get me to leave her alone."

He closed his eyes to keep himself from seeing his own face now, the tiny white scar covered mostly by his eyebrow so he was the only one who could see it. As he shook his head, trying to push away the image, he couldn't seem to stop shaking it. He started to thrash, jerking back and forth. Yanking against the hold of the mirror, he shoved against Dona's grip, shrugging her off. It was going to let him go. The strength of his rage would be enough to break even Hell's grip on him. The room would be consumed in flame and simply explode from it.

"You bitch. *You fucking...stupid...bitch.*" He screamed, roared at the image, wanted to be free so he could beat on it. Not just break it into pieces. He'd grind the shards to dust under his feet, even if it cut him. The blood would mingle with the dust and it would be justice. "I would have done anything to stay with you and you were a stupid...loser...junkie...whore. Tell this fucking...thing...to...LET ME GO!"

Dona's touch came back, rested on his back. He fought, railed, screamed endlessly as she said nothing, just stood behind him as a silent witness. It seemed to take a long while, but at length he became self-aware again, enough to feel her soft stroking on his skin, the way it seemed to be easing the compression in his chest, the burning in his throat and behind his eyes. It helped him get a grip and stop, gasping at his exertions.

"Look at yourself. Look." Her voice resonated through his upper body because she pressed her mouth between his shoulders, sliding her hands around to stroke his chest and belly. Long, soothing motions with a hint of nails.

A tall man with murder in his expression, his body layered with cold sweat and his muscles taut, wanting to destroy something with them.

"You said you didn't believe you could have a true Mistress," she whispered, kissing the base of his neck, making him close his eyes. "That you didn't believe in the fantasy of it. Jonathan denies you the reality. He's the angry little boy acting out, terrified, hiding in the closet, afraid his foster mother will find and beat him again. Or worse, not care that he's there, as if he's nothing, as if his existence doesn't matter."

"Stop it."

"No. You said it yourself. Think of what you made of yourself. You *are* strong. You're not garbage." She slid under his arm and was between him and that mirror now. When she lifted her hands, laid them on either side of his face, they seemed so fragile. He could break her fingers with barely any pressure and yet she seemed to have no fear of him when he was like this. When he was so enraged he feared himself, what he was capable of doing. "The only thing you lack is the courage to love, to forgive. That's the only thing that gives Jonathan power over your soul. That's what turns all those good things to poison. Let the little boy go and become the fine man I know is in my arms. Forgive."

"This can't be forgiven. Not ever."

"Are you talking about your mother? Or yourself?"

She was gone. His hands were free and the glass shattered, as if the brief interlude was just a passing dream and now time had resumed, the mirror feeling the impact of his fists. Blood bloomed on his knuckles.

The shadows in the surrounding mirrors swirled, a heavy fog that spilled out of the glass and poured into the room, black and silver, twisting together like the bodies of charred trees, touching his nose with the acrid smell of burning flesh. It warned him that something was coming, something that was at the heart of all of it. What had brought him here, the foundation of everything else. He knew enough to try and close his eyes, but he couldn't.

There were crimes that damned a man the moment they were committed. The soul always knew it. After that, nothing evil he did mattered. The black magic of this place wouldn't let him have the escape of seeing Dona this time. The mirrors clustered around him like the walls of a coffin, dancing out of the way only when he struck out at them.

Then his fists stopped in midair, clenched, unable to strike. For he was surrounded by her. By so many different images of her.

Eliza.

"You met Eliza when you were with your last foster mother. Your first true love. You were seventeen."

Eliza had been fifteen, and that's how he saw her now. Straight blonde hair, blue eyes. It was suddenly so pathetically obvious why he had stayed with Lauren longer than the other Mistresses he had manipulated. That same purity in her glance. Not the sickness infecting his own soul that made him such a good match for his foster mothers, so capable of manipulating them. He'd manipulated Lauren, but he'd never touched the core of her, because she was a grown woman who had been strong and clean enough that the filth of his soul hadn't been able to completely break her. Eliza hadn't been so lucky.

"You can't make me look at her. You can't." He dropped to a squat on the ground, his hands tight over his head. He wouldn't look at it. He'd be damned first.

*Careful, Nathan. There are no metaphors in Hell.*

The smoke cleared. He recognized the irony in the combination of smoke and mirrors, but he still wouldn't lift his head. Not until he felt the brush of Dona's leg against his side.

He exploded into motion, seizing her so in less than a blink he had her on her back, his body arched over hers, hands pinning her wrists to the ground, sitting on her hips to hold her down.

Her eyes were wide, startled, telling him she hadn't anticipated that move. Nor had some other power, if the rumble that went through the floor told him anything. It gave him the fleeting uneasy feeling of a lover about to confront the father of the village virgin he was ravishing. He didn't care. Let whatever demons that dwelled in this place come get him. He wasn't going to be torn open and left to bleed. He'd go down fighting.

His chest rose and fell, not from the effort of pinning a woman half his size, but the reaction of a man being chased over a long distance by things he knew he'd never outrun.

155

He'd keep running until he couldn't run further, though. When he went for her lips, she bit him. Snarling, he settled for her throat, biting her back, suckling on the skin to mark her as his, tasting her with his tongue, pressing his cock hard against her belly, letting her feel how much he wanted to fuck her. He could rape her, but as much as he hated having it pointed out by her earlier, he didn't work that way. He wanted her to command him, to arouse her so much she couldn't deny her own need. Her breasts pressed against his upper abdomen. He hated that corset. Letting go of her hands, he reached down and yanked the cups out of the way so he could grip the full curves, feel the press of her nipples in his palms.

"I want to see you come." His voice was rough, pleading to his own ears.

"I'll grant that wish." Those sorceress's eyes, looking up at him, told him a blink before it happened that he'd never had the upper hand at all.

The world spun and he was on his knees, ten feet away from her. He wanted to howl. Dona was still there, her corset dipped down like a waist cincher, showing those luscious breasts fully. When he tried to move forward, he was brought up short. He had manacles on his biceps and wrists and they were chained to an eyebolt in the floor, as if he were an animal in truth. As she studied him with that remote expression that saw everything, he felt vicious despair at it, at the way he felt so close to understanding one moment, close to getting into her head and yet yanked away in the next blink. The mirrors still rotated, but at the moment they were mercifully blank.

He wanted his hands on her thighs, his mouth and body close to hers. She came to him, cupped his face, let him catch his lips briefly on her wrist, the curve of her palm. Then she strolled across the chamber, back to that old Victorian fainting couch, complete with gold tassels over the carved wood and rich tapestry-patterned fabric. Tracing her hand over the top of one breast, she paused, her gaze going somewhere behind Nathan.

156

"Come," she said imperiously. "I wish you to service me."

Nathan stiffened as two men walked past him. Both were specimens of physical perfection, muscled, oiled, cocks erect. Each had an identical harness on his cock. A painfully tight chain ran from the base of it through the cleft of the muscular buttocks and hooked to the firmly buckled waist strap. In the front, there was a series of straps fastened with a metal stud in an overlapping point on the cock harness. They fanned out over the shaved pubic area in a sunburst design studded to the waist strap, measured exactly to keep the cock pulled up high.

One of the men had dark hair rippling down his back. The other's locks were almost white, so they were like yin and yang. As they turned, he saw one had wholly white eyes and the other black, both appearing to be blind, finding her by her voice only.

"Dona, no. I wanted—"

"To bring me fulfillment yourself? I don't think so. You prefer to tease women, not bring them true pleasure." She reached out, caressed and stroked the cock of the white-haired man now standing at her side. Bending, he finished unlacing the corset all the way down the front as she fondled him, wrapping her fist around his cock. "You could never surrender yourself, never give yourself so wholly over to a Mistress's pleasure."

She touched the thigh of the other man, standing on the opposite side of her. "Get me wet with your mouth," she purred the command. "I want to straddle that big cock of yours."

"Yes, Mistress." He moved to obey. Nathan watched, furious and confused, as the man knelt. The man waited for her to drape her legs gracefully on his shoulders and then he tore the crotch of the pants with one powerful movement that made her gasp. When he put his lips to work, Dona arched against the loveseat, her mouth opening in pleasure.

"Working you up has gotten me so hot," she said, her voice catching, lips curving in a smile of self-absorbed pleasure. "We're entitled to our coffee breaks down here, you know. When it serves a purpose."

In the world he'd left, if a Mistress introduced such a measure into the game, he'd counter it with a strategy of his own. Sulking petulance or feigned jealousy, whatever suited the purpose of making her think she was able to manipulate his emotions.

As she arched the man became more enthusiastic, his head moving between her legs, his muscular back rippling. The other man spread open the corset and framed her full breasts in his hands before moving to suckle her nipples. Nathan felt the heat of her response like a wave encompassing him.

He didn't want to watch other men pleasure his Mistress, but she was right. Darkness held him, seeking her desire only as a way to control her. Desolately, he realized he hadn't earned the right to do what these men were doing. With them she could lose herself in that haze that women found from just the simplest of touches upon their much more sensitized skin.

He wanted to do that for her, wanted to discover what minute changes of position would drive her higher, bring her to a climax so elevated it would shatter them both. Something entered into his conflicting feelings at this moment like a new flavor of wine he'd never tried before, bitter and sweet both, the kind of taste one kept drinking even as he wondered if he liked it.

Despite the fact he was undeserving, he found himself straining against his bonds, needing her to know, wanting her to see.

Her lips parted, tongue coming out to stroke them in a way he wanted to emulate. Her eyes were heavy-lidded when they focused on him. The flare in her eyes hit him like a punch in the gut. Her pleasure was being driven by him watching. The click of that connection eased the barbed wire around his heart, but not the aching lust, the fury to drive them away and serve her alone. Her desire was obviously rising as he raged against his chains, her eyes sliding over the slick bunched muscles in his shoulders and thighs as he tried to free himself. Curving up again into the blond's face, she moaned as he apparently thrust his tongue more deeply inside her.

"Oh...Nathan..." When she murmured his name, he wanted to weep. "You please your Mistress so much." Her voice drifted off and came back. "The look in your eyes, wanting me so much. You understand that's up to me, don't you? That's what submission is about. Your Mistress knows how to please you. Your cock is so hard right now. I can see it from here."

"Yes, Mistress," he groaned, as if her attention had physically clamped around it like her fist. "God...please, let me..."

"Your Mistress wants to fuck you. Wants to be fucked by you. But you have something to face first."

He shook his head. No. *No.* But even as he rejected it, he knew his capitulation was inevitable. He'd do anything for her if she asked it like this and she knew it. Women had tried to manipulate him before, but this wasn't that. As his Mistress, Dona was demanding that he face what he didn't want to face. He had no choice but to do it, because he had to obey her. His heart told him he did.

Dropping to one knee, he bowed his head in surrender.

"Yes," he whispered. And shuddered.

# Chapter Ten

There was some pleasure in the fact that Yin and Yang went away like a puff of smoke the moment he acquiesced. There was little pleasure in what came next. His Mistress, laced back in her armor, circling him the way the mirrors were doing, the images of Eliza stalking him.

As mouthwatering and sexy as the outfit was designed to be, something deeper in his soul than lust had wanted to see Dona unadorned by anything but her own lovely skin. Unshielded as he felt at this moment.

"She loved you so much. You wanted to love her. So desperately."

Nathan stared at the pretty young face, the tiny hoop earrings in her lobes, the careful application of makeup. A girl becoming a woman with cautious steps.

He wanted to touch her face and suddenly he could, or at least his hands were free to touch the surface of the glass. It gave way beneath his touch, almost like the softness of skin.

"I didn't mean to hurt her. If I could..." He closed his hand into a fist, pulled it away. "It doesn't matter. I can't."

"No, you can't. It does matter, though. True regret and remorse can be powerful catalysts for change."

He turned to find Dona, but she had an annoying way of being out of his view when she wanted him to focus on something else. All he saw were more mirrors.

"She loved you so much that you thought she was weak."

The images began chasing one another through all the mirrors, above, below, all around. Showing him things he didn't want to see.

"She wasn't weak."

"No," Dona agreed. "She was a young girl in love for the first time, confused by her hormones and feelings, a girl who got herself involved with a boy who already knew how to hustle and outmaneuver women three times his age. You didn't believe in her devotion. It fascinated and sickened you. So you started rebelling against it in small ways, testing it. Seeing if it was real, this phenomenon you'd never experienced. You weren't merciful enough to cut her loose. You wanted what she had to offer even though you didn't understand it. Evil fears what it doesn't understand. If it can't prove it a lie, it destroys it and calls it weak."

He wanted to look away, but invisible hands that felt like reptilian skin clamped down on his head and neck. Making him turn from one image to another, his body unable to move on its own, a marionette.

Dona walked before the panel of mirrors, her fingers traveling along the base of the glass, her head tilted up, watching, though he had the odd feeling she was able to see his face at the same moment she was watching the scenes play out around them, shaming him before her. The women he had been with did not know this side of him until he allowed them to know. She knew it all, was watching it with him. That made it worse.

"First, it was typical things," Dona continued. "Telling her you'd call her and not doing so deliberately. Canceling a date at the last moment and then making sure she saw you somewhere having fun without her. Just when she was hurt and angry enough to break up with you, you'd come back with a smooth move that usually takes men years to learn. Showing up at her door unexpectedly with a planned picnic, or bringing her flowers during a class where all her friends would see. That little pendant you bought her with the unicorn etched on it. Taking her on a bus to the equestrian championship."

"She loved horses," he murmured.

"Yes. She treasured that day, probably because she sensed how much you genuinely enjoyed it, surprising yourself. You honed your best seduction skills on her, Jonathan. With your foster mothers, you learned to manipulate and deceive using their weaknesses of character. With Eliza, you learned how to turn a woman's greatest strength into her greatest liability. Her capacity to love. She was your experiment, teaching you how far you could push a woman's love to breaking point and then reel her back in. As if you were the ultimate deep-sea fisherman of love."

She drew out the syllables, mocking him now. Nathan clenched his teeth. "It wasn't like that."

"Most of it was, yes. There were parts that weren't. Like here." The image in the mirror froze and he was looking at himself at the championship with Eliza. She was watching the winning horse complete a jump, her eyes shiny with amazement, absorbed in the beauty of the animal and rider. She was lost in a young girl's dream that it could be her on that horse, making those jumps, becoming something more than she'd expected to be. He leaned back in his seat while she leaned forward, his seventeen-year-old self just as captivated by her, for virtually the same reason.

"It freaked you out, big time, how you felt that day. After that, your games got worse. Your tests more intense. Hot one day, cold the next, you went from fisherman to orchestra maestro, learning to make her emotions perform the composition you wished." Dona turned, cocked her head. "You successfully graduated into a sexual predator at seventeen. That's very impressive."

"Are you done yet?" He tried to sound angry, unaffected, but he thought he was going to go insane if he had to watch the images another moment. His muscles were trembling at the effort to loose the invisible bindings which were once again thwarting his overwhelming need to look away.

"Not even close, apparently." She turned her attention back to the mirrors. "She entered her junior year an entirely different girl. Nervous, high-strung, completely dependent on you. When you told her to get on her knees and suck off one of your so-called friends at a party on a bet, she didn't even hesitate, though she cried the whole time. They thought it was just her eyes watering from the size of his dick, but you knew."

The image came up, stark and brutal, the football player's meaty hand on her delicate head, fingers curled in her hair. Jonathan sat in the background watching, acknowledging the ribald jokes of his friends egging her on like it was a beer-chugging competition. Calls of "me next" were being mouthed.

"Stop..." He strangled it out, fought the restraint with real fervor. Dona appeared next to him in that quick blink of reality that seemed to staple time together and erase transitions, making everything more intense. Her fingers curled in his ear, pinched, her voice a hiss.

"We're not stopping. Not until it's enough. One of the most important parts of punishment is reliving your crimes with complete awareness. The soldiers that decapitated children in Rwanda, it drives them mad to understand the depths of their own barbarity. Down here, insanity isn't a defense. It's not even original. Look and tell me why you shouldn't receive the most severe punishment possible for doing this to a girl whose only crime was loving you?"

She turned on her heel, went back to the mirrors. He watched the horrifying scene play out as Eliza was passed to two other boys to perform the same act. While he couldn't stop the flow of images, it didn't stop him from wishing it. Wishing he didn't feel every word Dona had said in his gut like a knife wound, bleeding truth.

"That was the first weekend she tried to kill herself. Her parents never even suspected you were the cause, because in their presence you were so solicitous of her every need. You were getting bored of the game, though. That's what you told yourself. So without a word to Eliza and only a brief note to your foster mother so she wouldn't bother looking for you, on the day of your graduation you picked up your diploma, drove out of town and never looked back."

Her voice continued its brutal laceration of his memories. "Your ability to love, if you ever had it, was annihilated at that point. Nathan Polinsky stopped existing and Jonathan Powell took control. Casual dates were never casual for you. You staked out your quarry and went after her with a hunter's instinct. Every time you succeeded, you wanted stronger prey. The stronger the better. You would take them all down, prove that none of them could take advantage of Jonathan Powell. It's your addiction. When you see a woman, you immediately start gauging her defenses, her strengths, figuring out how to work your way through them."

She turned and faced him, that terrible memory replaying behind her in graphic, stark detail. He tried to block it out, tried to just focus on Dona's eyes, the movement of her lips, but he couldn't ignore Eliza's tears. *She'd trusted him.*

That was her fault. He hadn't asked her to love him so much she sacrificed her self-respect. She should have known he was bullshit and turned her back on him, gone with one of those right-side-of-the-track guys whose worst offense would be the cliché of taking her virginity in the back of his car and giving her flowers afterward.

"Eliza truly loved you. She let you destroy her because she sensed how much you needed her. She was too young and pure to understand, but it didn't make her love less noble. We believe love is strong enough to overcome everything, but that's not exactly true. Love endures. It can rise out of the ashes of a destroyed relationship to be the foundation for the next one. But you don't love, Jonathan. You choose a woman only to make her suffer." The mirror images faded away, just as Eliza had faded out of his life, forever gone.

The thought of her had lingered for so many years, until he'd finally locked her in a room of his subconscious, ignoring her no matter how often she beat on the door and screamed.

Eventually he'd piled enough debris on her to silence her. Until Dona unearthed her again.

He'd tried to love Eliza even harder than he'd tried to love Lauren. Perhaps in both he'd sensed the key to his salvation, something that could be his if he could just get past his fears. He had failed, both times. In the end he just couldn't trust either woman enough.

Sick at heart, confused, he nevertheless lifted his gaze to Dona, pinned her with a defiant look. "I didn't choose *you*. You came for me." Inside, he wondered if somehow that would make it different this time, cause it to end differently. Wished the thought didn't tear at his insides with self-doubt and loathing.

"You're exactly right. I did."

Suddenly she was back on that couch, sprawled like the temptress she was. Her thighs spread open, showing him the glistening folds, her body entirely, blessedly naked, her arm lying lazily above her head, indolent. "Do you think you can pleasure me far better than those two did?"

A confusing thicket of lust, anger and need rose up in him like the rasp of thorns on the inside of his chest. A need to get rid of his pain by immersing himself in her body. "Hell, yes," he growled.

"You are arrogant, Nathan." Her lips curved. "I do like that about you. Come fuck your Mistress."

\* \* \* \* \*

He stumbled as he moved forward, finding his ankles manacled on a close chain. He had to make short, shuffling steps to get to her, underscoring his servitude, reminding him that his desires and needs were tempered by her Will.

As if she knew he understood the lesson, the bonds were gone. He stood before her, naked as she was, the two of them staring at each other. Despite the moment of bravado, he was still off balance, shaky inside and out from facing Eliza. He

165

noticed then that Dona was trembling too, though he couldn't imagine why she'd be nervous about this moment. Unless this moment was different. As he looked into her eyes, he saw it was. She was lying on her back, waiting for him to come to her. Waiting to take his body onto hers, allow him to spread her legs and sink into her. After all the terrible things she'd seen of his soul, she was opening her own, giving him a moment of her own vulnerability, and he had no idea why.

He took one step and then another, as careful as if he was still bound at the ankles. Her eyes, the very energy that surrounded her, captivated him, tortured him and yet brought him a sense of security he'd never had before and didn't understand now. She anticipated everything, so he didn't have to pretend anything.

Yet she shivered at his approach.

It made him want to give her everything, be a far better man than he'd ever desired to be before, even though he knew it was too late. Instead of falling on her like a rutting bull, he knelt and put his lips to the tender arch of one bare foot.

Had he ever let himself savor a woman? Breathe in her essence like this while her body lay before him like a gift beyond measure? Press his mouth to her skin amid the punishments of Hell, rub his cheek against her ankle like an affectionate tomcat and see her lips curve in a distracted smile. In the vast knowledge he had of the way women's physical responses were inextricably tied to the emotional, he understood her body could be violently aroused by that one touch on her foot. There were no individual body parts on a woman. Everything was connected, every touch felt at several different levels, a mystery that a man could comprehend, be grateful for, but never understand himself.

"Nathan." She spoke his name in a whisper, the name his soul knew. Raising her arms, she looked at him with eyes of rich brown earth, welcoming him. "Did you ever have a pet, my lovely slave?"

He shook his head. "I had a friend with a cat. When I was a kid. It seemed to like me."

"Did you like petting the cat?"

"I did. She…" A painful smile came to him at the thought that the feline had been a female. Dona gave him an answering soft smile on her lips that said she'd followed his thoughts easily. "It was nice, petting her."

"Have you ever thought about the way a cat or dog is so willing to touch and be touched? Be my pet. Let me touch you, pet you."

"I haven't earned this gift, Mistress."

"I have." There was a sudden fierceness to her, a ripple of something that suggested that this moment had not been planned as part of the program. However, he was learning there were tremendous benefits to not arguing with a Mistress.

He put his knee on the couch and lurched, catching himself as their surface moved like a waterbed. They were back in the oasis under a Van Gogh starry night sky. While they floated on a human-sized lily pad, smaller clusters drifted by, their white blooms scenting the air. The night was filled with frog warblings.

He caught himself on his elbow to keep from falling on her, which put his other hand in the perfect place to cup her face, his thumb tracing her collarbone. One of her hands was at his ribs, the other at his hip, steadying him as he got accustomed to the sensual undulation of the water at their every movement. The edges of the pad cupped up, keeping the water from them.

"How *do* you do that?"

"I don't. Not always. After so many years, I anticipate His thoughts and plan, the settings He gives me, but sometimes He alters what I imagine. I'd intended you to make love to me on the couch. He liked this better."

"So do I." He was suddenly, intensely aware of the fact his body was laid upon hers full length, her thighs cradling his hips, nothing between them. "Would you like me to switch places, my lady, so you can ride me to your pleasure?"

"No." Her eyes were luminous, filled with the stars above, making him dizzy. "I don't need to be on top to be your Mistress. After all, you're waiting on my permission, aren't you?"

He couldn't deny it. "May I kiss you?"

"Not yet." She tilted her hips. With the pressure of her hands on his buttocks, she angled him so his head pushed in, sunk into her wet heat like the answer to every fear or question he'd ever had. He couldn't help resting his forehead on hers, swamped by the sensation. Emotions flooded him, along with the desire to move.

He stiffened, lifting his head. "I didn't...Mistress, forgive me. Protection... Do you need it here? I know it's a little late to be thinking of it..."

She framed his face with her hands, her voice husky. "No. This is a place where protection isn't an option, in any form. It pleases me that you thought of protecting me, though."

"I wish I could destroy the part of me you call Jonathan." He blurted it out. "You were right, a moment ago. It's so deep inside me..." The sound that he forced out of his throat was too harsh to be a laugh, too bitter to be a sob. "I'm never going to deserve you."

"Hush," she said, her fingers brushing his lips. She moved her hands, cupped her palms over the small of his back. Tightening her legs on the swell of his buttocks, she lifted up to him, taking him more deeply and presenting her breasts to his suddenly dry mouth. "Move inside of me. Slow. Strong."

He obeyed. It was torturous, feeling her walls slide along his length, convulse against him, the firm pressure of her tiny clit against his pubic area, the feel of her body everywhere it touched him. Stroking, gripping, moonlight on the arch of her throat. The gratifying sounds of her increasing breaths, her cry of pleasure as he bent his head and suckled her breasts in turn, bit her throat, trying in every way he knew to increase her pleasure.

He wanted to make her climax as shattering as he was sure his was going to be, if she permitted him the reward. Each slow and even stroke made it far more difficult to hold back, particularly when she showed no signs of letting him release. But even more than the desire to climax, he wanted this moment to go on forever, bask in her pleasure at his touch and their joining. It was too open on her face to be feigned, too obvious in the clutch of her limbs.

He wished he could kiss her mouth, that final and most precious gift of intimacy. Though he was tempted past bearing to do so with her so close beneath him, her chin rubbing his head as he suckled her again, nipped her, he didn't. For she had forbidden him to kiss her. He didn't want to do anything to stop this moment.

It brought him back to moments with other Mistresses, moments somewhat like this when their love and response had been offered as freely as Dona's was now. He could see those moments now with new eyes. Every drop of love freely offered could have been another restorative to his sick soul. Healing had always been within his reach, but his fears had been greater.

With the truths his Mistress of Redemption had shown him came the knowledge of all he had done and all he must do to make it right to earn the love of a Mistress like Dona. But he didn't want one *like* Dona. He wanted *her*. Was that ridiculous, like the soldier falling for his nurse?

Maybe it was a twisted sort of Stockholm Syndrome, or an attachment to the first woman who'd offered justice and love in the same touch. His gut, which had been well honed to identify the nuances of a woman's moods to take advantage of her, sensed what lay between the two of them was far more than that. She'd said they were soul mates, hadn't she?

When she tightened her muscles on him, he gasped, his fingers curling into her dark hair. "Mistress."

"Harder now. Stronger. Let me feel how strong you are," she whispered. "How savage your passion can be when it's unleashed honestly."

He didn't need a second invitation or further explanation. Scooping his arm under her waist, he clamped her to him, held both of their weights on one arm as he surged into her. Thrusting his cock hard and deep, he watched her eyes glaze, her mouth open, that beautiful neck arch back even further, inviting. Her fingers dug into his buttocks and he didn't disappoint her, continuing the deep thrusts, fully withdrawing on each stroke to tease her sensitive opening and clit, feeling how she slid slickly over him. Their boat rocked, adding to the sensation with the uncontrolled response to their passion. The world tilted around them.

"My name." He suddenly had that one desperate demand. "Please."

"Nathan. My heart. My soul mate." It came to her lips so easily, he knew it had to be truth. She knew the purest part of who he was. He was here between her legs now, giving her all of himself, all she would allow. With an overwhelming desire he'd never allowed himself to feel, he *wanted* to give it all. He didn't want to be afraid, just wanted to give everything to her, even if she slashed him to ribbons. As they drew closer to climax, the power of it immersed him. He could tell she was experiencing the same connection. Light was rising, surrounding them both as if they were about to detonate and create a new star.

He bent his head, fully intending to capture her lips with his own, feeling that he could dare it now. However, her hand came up at the last moment, pressing against his mouth. He had to content himself with sucking on those fingertips, licking the tender crevices. Suckling on her palm, he fastened his teeth on her wrist pulse as she convulsed beneath him, cried out, her legs tightening on him.

"Go...now..." It was barely coherent, but he thanked whatever Powers there were for her mercy as his cock pulsed in response to the release of her pussy. He jetted deep inside her, groaning as her body gripped him like a fist. He made love to her, fucked her, gave and took from her in every way possible to bring her pleasure, his thighs taut beneath her questing fingertips, shoulder muscles standing out as he gave her every ounce of strength he had. Serving her pleasure to the last vibration of her climax, he thought of nothing else but that, no future plans or past failures. There was just now. Their natural green boat swayed with them, adding to the pleasure, a rhythm controlled by a power far beyond both of them and far more ancient.

It was a good thing that Nathan could not see into her the way she could see into him at this moment. Immersed in his thoughts, Dona knew she would have abandoned everything required of her just to stay in this moment with him, her arms and legs holding him, the quiet sounds of the night surrounding them. As he slowed, responding to the languid cadence of her body signaling her completion, his chest rose and fell against hers. When he lowered his head, she closed her eyes and felt the touch of his lips against her cheek as he nuzzled her. She knew everything inside him. His wonder. His love. At this moment, she held Nathan in her arms. Jonathan wasn't even a whisper of darkness in the pure light that filled them.

*God, help me be cruel enough to help him. Don't let me be selfish. I'm getting so lost in him, I'm not sure what the right path is anymore.*

After all they had shared and all she had done to him, Nathan was amazed at how light and delicate she felt in his arms. He tightened his arms around her because he sensed she needed that strength, the feel of his wanting her. He wouldn't ever stop. He wanted to tell her, but something in her face kept him quiet. As they finished with intense, lingering aftershocks, his brow came to rest on hers, his mouth only inches from those tempting lips. He wondered mazily if she was so light because he was holding her soul. It contented him to believe it.

Pressing his lips to her shoulder, he closed his eyes as he sensed the shadows hovering at the edges of his own soul, waiting. His foster mothers, his mother. Eliza. How could he have Dona when there was so much hatred and bitterness in him? "The world is so dark," he murmured. "You told me there's hope. This is the only moment of hope I can imagine, but you're not ready to give me your love. So there's only despair for me, isn't there?"

*Because without you, I can't be healed. But if I'm with you...* He would destroy her. The thought terrified him. He thought he might rather suffer the fires of Hell than know he'd done that to her. For as invincible as she seemed, he knew she wasn't.

She was quiet beneath him, stretching her neck up to nuzzle his throat with her nose. He sensed her hesitation, as if she was considering many different issues that he did not understand. He waited on her Will, too full of the past few moments and too fearful of the next to speak further.

\* \* \* \* \*

Darkness could be comforting, bringing a floating sensation. There was a flash of light that hurt his eyes. A sense of apprehension came with that light, then there was a murmur of sound. The light receded, became soft blue, green. The smell of grass touched his senses and he was staring up into layers of blue and green leaves with soft filtering silver lights.

Peace, such as he'd never known and never imagined could exist, filled him. It became his blood, his breath. He could lie here forever and it would be okay. Everything he'd done wrong, every shortcoming he'd recognized or imagined in himself, every self-doubt, every hurt, it was all forgiven. Everything was centered, simple. It therefore made perfect sense that he felt her hand in his. Looking over, he saw she lay beside him, both of them naked. It wasn't sexual, it just was. Her hair was loose and soft, so he reached out and touched it, held it in his hands and buried his face in it as she circled her arms around his head, held him, rocked with him. They rolled, tumbled over and over together on the soft blanket of the ground, a fun, gentle exercise of movement. The tangling of limbs, the rubbing together of bodies. When they stopped, they were on the slope of a hill. Sitting up, he kept her in the span of one arm as he looked around. They'd been lying in a grove of trees, but just below the green earth gave way to the silver plateau of a lake framed by snow-capped mountains, sculpted with lines of past melting waters. A canvas entirely sculpted by Nature. Untouched by human hands, everything tranquil, still…

By the lake, a lion came to drink, an antelope rubbing up against his flank, dancing away with playful lack of fear as he grumbled at it as a cat might do. A stone's throw away, several rabbits lay quietly in their warren, watching it all. Ducks and their young moved across the water.

"I've never felt…is this one of the illusions of this place, Dona? Is what I'm feeling real? What *am* I feeling?"

"Contentment. Pure, simple contentment. A desire for nothing except what's around you already. No desire to do harm." When Dona reached up, touched his face, he pressed his lips to her wrist, holding the kiss there, savoring her skin, feeling the fingers of her other hand move along his cock and rest against his thigh. A natural, easy touch, freely exchanged with no tension or expectation. As much as he enjoyed the feel of lust, this was somehow an even stronger type of desire, even in its tranquility.

"Can we stay here forever?"

A shadow crossed her face. "No. This is Eden. We can only visit for special purposes, short moments. Humans are forbidden to live here until they achieve full enlightenment. That's where there's hope, Nathan. Not only in the destination, but in the journey to get there. The promise of it."

\* \* \* \* \*

"Tell me one dream you had."

He begged for it, wanting some key to understanding her. "Big or small."

"Had?" She lifted a brow. "We dream here too. We do nothing but dream."

His Mistress rested her chin on her knuckles as they sat cross-legged, shoulder to shoulder, staring down the hill at the gateway to Eden. The being who had temporarily allowed them entry was back on guard, the sword like a flickering star.

They were like two kids in a treehouse, sharing confidences. After experiencing Eden together, Nathan thought the bond between them right now felt like a quiet knowledge of one another down to the soul, far beyond sexual interest, even beyond man and woman. No human could have remained unmoved in such a place. He had been given this glimpse, not just of the Garden, but of her.

"I used to get poison ivy every year, in the spring," she said at last. "Sometimes it itched so badly... The best thing for it is wet compresses. Just a wet cloth laid over it. There's this first moment, just a blink, when the cloth touches your skin. It's so intense it almost feels like an orgasm and you want to scratch so badly. Then the coolness is there, taking it all away. Miraculous, just something natural that makes it feel better. I always have this fantasy of a man who loves me doing that. Putting those wet compresses on my ankles, this look of concern in his eyes. Changing them out when needed. Telling me not to get up, that he'll take care of it." Her gaze shifted to him. "His kisses would be like that terrible burning itch at the first contact, melting away into something natural that feels like contentment, everything I need." A corner of her mouth lifted. "It wasn't what you expected one of my fantasies to be, was it?"

He couldn't help but grin, lift a shoulder. She bumped him with her own.

"Typical man. Tell me one of your dreams…or fantasies."

The question took him by surprise, mainly because he couldn't remember any from his life other than momentary prurient things about a woman and sex. Something stirred in the mud of his subconscious, but like those shadows that kept flitting in the edges of his vision, he didn't want to look closely at them. The question…hurt. The other things she'd pulled from him—anger, anxiety, uncertainty and confusion—they had been difficult, but he couldn't seem to answer this question.

"I don't know," he said at last. "When you were talking, I thought…it might be nice to be the type of man who deserved to kneel at your feet and put those compresses on." He stared down at Eden. "I'll never be that kind of person, will I? Ever. I mean, I want to at this moment, but in a few minutes, I'll be afraid and then angry. I'll be angry at you and I won't know why… I can almost feel it getting ready to start up again. If I can't… If something like feeling Eden can't make me good for longer than five minutes, then what…"

"Nathan." Her touch stilled his sudden desperation.

"You always call me that when you're going to be kind…or your most cruel."

She nodded, acknowledging it. "Jonathan will never get there because Jonathan is not you. He's not your soul. Nathan can, because he *is* your soul. Nathan is braver than Jonathan and knows what he has to do. This is a place for the soul to clean off the disguises we've placed upon it. It's not pretty, it's not easy. Jonathan is so firmly adhered, you've made him into your skin. To become Nathan alone, you're going to have to skin yourself alive."

"What I've done…" Eliza's blue tear-filled eyes were in his mind, torturing him even without the presence of the mirrors. Quiet despair took him. Resignation. "She killed herself. Killed herself because of me, three months after I left. I got drunk when I heard, tied one on for a week. Cursed her.

Even snuck back into town and pissed on her tombstone, screamed at her."

*Passed out on the grave and woke up with his face stained with a night's worth of tears and the taste of vomit in his throat.*

"I know."

"Forgiveness isn't possible, is it?" There was a weight on his heart as he said the words, a weight he was sure would keep him pinned down forever.

"No, it isn't. Not initially." Her fingers touched his jaw. Somehow she had the strength he lacked, though he felt as if his head was heavier than the world's sorrows. She lifted it, made him meet her gaze. "Redemption is. Payment for your crimes, acceptance of that burden."

He saw in her eyes that she had walked that path as well.

"When it's true," she said quietly, "when the debts have been accepted into your heart and paid, then there is forgiveness."

"From God?" His lip curled up, half derisive, but he knew it was a mask for hope.

"Yes, from all that is God. From your own soul, which is the part of God that dwells within you. You come home to yourself and to the Great Lord and Lady, whatever name you choose to give Them. You discover what drives the redemption, the justice, the forgiveness. The Constant."

"What's that?"

"Love. Faith. They are one, for they're inseparable."

He swallowed, managed a scoff that came off like a sob. "I don't have that, do I?"

"I love you. I believe in you."

"Because we're soul mates."

"Yes and no." She cocked her head. "I don't think the feeling that soul mates have is a biological imperative we have no control over. I think we're matched because we chose one another, back when our souls were new. No more than babies, because babies understand everything."

He swallowed. No one loved him. No one ever had, and he'd done nothing since the realization to make himself more loveable. What could he have done, anyway? He'd started his life with a black mark over him. *There's something wrong with this one. Its mother didn't want it.* Why not throw such an infant on a refuse heap, let it go back to dust unnamed, rather than making him suffer through a life branded with the tearing pain of that knowledge? Perhaps that was the true secret of the tree of good and evil. Adam's and Eve's eyes were opened, and they knew then they would suffer through pain. Their children and children's children would be subjected to unspeakable evil because their Father truly didn't give a shit. They'd simply been Play-Doh toys to amuse Him.

He didn't want the bitterness to overtake him, rob him of this moment. "Please... Will you say what you just said...one more time?"

She hesitated a moment, enough to warn him that what she was about to do wasn't necessarily something intended. When she leaned over, she stopped just before she reached his lips and looked into his eyes. "I love you, Nathan. I always will."

Then she kissed him. Not the brief brush he'd stolen from her in the beginning, but a full fusion of their mouths, her lips coaxing open his to tease him with her tongue, make him feel her need as well as his own.

Everything went away. There were no clothes, no piercings, no Hell, nothing. It was like they were back in the Garden again, only there were no forms. Just the feel of it surrounding them, the light of that sword a protective cocoon holding all of it in. No bindings kept his hands from her and yet he found he could not move until his Mistress gently closed her hands on his wrists and brought them to her waist. He touched her skin and more than her skin. He felt her body against his, but at the same time there were no barriers at all, as if his soul simply stepped into the light of hers. The Dona his eyes had seen all the time, the Goth Mistress of Hell with her red lips and dark-rimmed eyes, faded away. The disguise for her soul.

He nearly cried out at the flood of white light that poured into him, surrounded him, held him. It was like that poison ivy she had described, a moment of overwhelming craving for something before it melted into this. Contentment, peace, desire sated forever in nothing more than an embrace, in one kiss. He could almost feel the softness of her wings enfold him, the purity of her so strong he could no longer use vision to see her. He simply closed his eyes and kissed her back, kissed this beautiful spirit who was kissing him. He held her in his hands, held light as substance.

When she broke away and stood back from him, her eyes were wide, almost frightened. She was the Dona he knew physically, but so different. His soul knew her, knew things his rational mind did not understand and was already scrambling to hold, frightened of losing a grasp on them.

*We may not have Eden. But we have this.*

It was as clear in his head as if she'd spoken it. He saw it in her eyes.

"Dona, you…you're an ang—"

*You're my soul mate.*

He'd seen the movies where the elevator cable gave way, plunging the occupants into screaming terror. Suddenly the Garden was gone, the ground was gone and he dropped, tumbling into darkness. Dona dissipated before his eyes, her mouth open on a cry, perhaps a scream, as he fell…

# Chapter Eleven

## ❧

Cold stone. He was on cold, wet stone. He got to his feet in complete darkness, feeling off balance from the lack of a visual anchor. Dona hadn't been in control of this. He'd seen it in her eyes, the fear, the guilt. She'd broken some type of rule. At the thought, suddenly where he was and what was about to happen to him were irrelevant.

"Dona!" He shouted her name. At first he only heard silence. Then he wished for silence.

It was a moaning, like a lonesome wind through a dark forest at night, only there was no wind, no forest. A tide of voices rising in a discordant symphony of despair, the keening punctuated by the occasional shriek of agony. The sound people made when fear overcame every rational thought so all that was left was the unstoppable need to scream.

"Dona!" He roared it, moving forward, stumbling blindly. "She didn't do anything wrong. It was me, my fault. Leave her alone. Dona, dammit, where are you?"

He fell, caught himself with a hand, felt rock stab his palm, but more importantly, he noted his fingers fluttered over nothing. He was on the edge of something and it was from that chasm the wailing was coming. It was far away, but not so far that the despair couldn't blast him like the heat of a furnace. Everything in him told him to back away, to scramble from that precipice. But Dona could be there. Dona might need him.

Snarling, he charged forward before he could lose his sense of direction. Intending to leap into open space, instead he yelped in surprise when he came up short, rammed hard into a surface like a brick wall that rapped him smartly on the forehead. It made him stagger back, his senses spinning.

179

"She's not there. Granted, she cheated there at the end, but since it was a compulsion of her heart, it was not a true deception. She wanted to let you understand your true self, even if for only a moment. I'm not inclined to punish her for that. It was an act of Fate. I suspect that my Lady's stubborn, meddling and yet usually right Will was also somehow involved. For you see, only your soul mate can bring your soul to the surface with a kiss."

Nathan blinked to find his surroundings had become illuminated. He was on a cliff top, a pillar of rock surrounded on all sides by an open chasm. The light came from a fire-like glow that emitted from the chasm, as if they floated on a sea of embers.

The voice came from a man squatting on bare feet not more than ten feet from him. "Man" came to Nathan's mind only because of His form. While the man rested on His knuckles in a familiar, mundane pose, the energy pulsing from Him was overwhelming, such that Nathan could do no more than obey the compulsion of his trembling legs to fall to his knees.

It was the light he had felt inside Dona, only this was the source, her light like the gift of one of its rays.

The man had pale skin, almost a silk-gray in the light. His long dark hair fell snarled over broad shoulders, the strands tangling in the upper curve of the gray silver-white feathered wings that were half spread, balancing Him, as much a part of His body as a bird's.

When He rose, His height was equal to Nathan's, but Nathan knew the stature of the Being before him had no ceiling. His form was merely convenient. He could not find the strength to rise to his feet before Him. There was no room for rational thought and therefore no room for deception. There was only emotion, pure raw. All that seemed to matter now was how badly he'd fucked up everything and how much he missed Dona. Needed her, even though he didn't deserve even to have a memory of her.

"We...belong together." Saying the words was a comfort. It was the only response he had the strength to manage.

"Since the beginning of time." Lucifer nodded, considering him. Nathan felt the terrible power in that look, underscored by the disturbing keening still rising up from the flames, more muted now. "But the time has to be right. You've found your soul again, with her help. But it doesn't absolve the crime. It does not pay your karmic debt. You haven't been fully redeemed, now have you?"

It flitted through him again, what he'd felt in her arms, joined with her. The shadows that represented the rage and darkness of his soul. The guilt at the things he'd done. The inability to forgive.

"That's not Dona's failing, though she'll think it is. If I returned you to Purgatory in a new body, you're likely to let the same fears guide your actions. If you met her in mortal life, you could destroy her as you have destroyed others."

*But I need her now...*

It was what his soul cried out, the soul that had begged for his mother.

*What's behind the mirror?*

No Dona now. Nothing but himself to answer the question. So what was the answer?

On his knees before what he knew was the Power behind everything, it was all as clear and simple as a mirror, ironically. The final true reflection was undeniable, like the feel of rain pounding on his skin. Dona had broken him down, broken him open. With this Being's power pouring into those raw wounds, truth came bubbling up like pus out of an infection. It was pathetic, a cliché. It wasn't that he hadn't always known it. It was the difference between hearing and knowing.

He knew what Dona's husband had thrown away, because he'd thrown it away a dozen times. But for the first time he felt the actual weight of all the things he'd been offered and spurned. A weight that had grown so gradually over time he hadn't realized everything he thought he was had been disintegrating beneath the tonnage, damaged beyond even Dona's ability to repair.

In the depths of his heart, he still believed women were evil. They had a power in them to make a man love them so much, but they would turn on him, use his love against him. Every time Dona had given him some slack, it had reared its head in him again, the need to teach them how it felt, his own brand of karmic justice. Rejecting every woman just as she gave him her love. Always wishing he could find his mother, do it to her. As if the vicious bitch had love to give. He would have done anything to keep her love. To not be abandoned to the demonic creatures that had masqueraded as his foster mothers.

He closed his eyes, bowed his head.

*Look in the mirror. Look behind your mother and what do you see? What do you see, Nathan?*

As an unloved and unwanted child, he'd started spinning those mirrors early. Now he was a man unworthy of a woman's love, a creation of his own making, full of anger and bitterness that he'd coated in charm and deception. All he wanted was for one woman to prove him wrong. To tear away all his weapons and shields, beat him to his knees before her, prove to him that he had no need of weapons or shields. Not with her.

But she had done it, hadn't she? Dona had done it. She could force him to trust, because he couldn't make the choice himself.

"Life has to be about that choice, or it isn't earned."

A new energy, like the Lord before him, but different. Different and yet together. He'd felt hints of both of Them in Dona's light. In that one touch, that one soft sentence, he crumbled to the rock, weeping. For now he felt a Mother's love, felt it as it was meant to be. Unconditional. Forgiving, even while administering justice. Always there. Never to be doubted. He'd never needed to doubt Her. She was Dona and every woman who'd let Light into their souls to love a man with all they had. All he'd ever wanted was to love a woman unconditionally, freely, and receive this gift in return. So that he'd never know loneliness and abandonment again.

"I'm sorry. I'm so sorry."

"I know." Her touch along his body was warm and simple, like a blanket. "You have to find the courage to make the choice. You belong together. She needs you, maybe even more than you need her."

He didn't have that kind of courage. He knew he didn't. Like a man with a terminal disease, only of the mind instead of the body, he knew where he would fail.

If he destroyed Dona, he knew without being told he'd damn himself forever. There were things that were beyond unforgivable. Meaning unfixable, and destroying one half of yourself, the best half, would certainly fall in that category.

"Find the quiet place in yourself, the center. Let down all your shields and simply be. Accept what is. To pay for your transgressions, you have to be willing to accept that payment will be made. You have to forgive yourself."

He thought of the tree where he'd hidden his treasures, thought of laying down a carpet of soft pine needles for Dona there. Her fingers would caress his head, his ears and jaw, pressing him down between her legs to make him service her. The trees above would be layers of blues and green like Eden, the peace of nature all around. With the passion he'd bring the peace. Part of him acting as a lover, suckling her cunt, the other part of him like a son worshipping at the Mother's womb, both aspects bringing fulfillment.

The fire-like glow and the feel of the cold stone returned. He was there with just Lucifer, the Lady's presence like a lullaby fading as he woke from sleep. Nathan pushed himself to his hands and knees, breathing deeply, hearing a silence in himself he'd never heard. A place of quiet, terrible truth.

Joey W. Hill

"I have to go to Hell, don't I?"

"I think so, yes." Lucifer answered him. "But that is your choice. You have performed well enough in Redemption to earn the right to another body."

A body with a soul still infected with enough corruption that he could simply end up here again. He could feel the darkness in him, confused but waiting to reorganize as soon as doubt, guilt and rage crept in.

"The time in Hell will be bad. You will pay through direct punishment for all that you've done to others. It will be far more than the pain you've suffered thus far. There is much of Jonathan in you still, so getting rid of his influence will not be pleasant. It will be agony."

Despair and pain knocked him back to the cold stone. It was every bad, anxious feeling he'd ever had magnified a thousand times, fears and terrors of the night he couldn't even imagine crowding in on him. He thrashed, struck out. Abruptly he was back on the cold stone, huddled in a fetal ball, sick to his stomach but unable to retch.

Lucifer regarded him with a dispassionate eye. "That was barely a tenth of what you will feel and I gave it to you for a blink of time. Do you still wish to undertake this course?"

Nathan managed to respond, his voice hoarse. "If I go to Hell, will she be safe from me?"

"Safer than if you don't."

He had his answer. *She needs you.*

"How long in Hell..." Nathan forced his lips to ask the question.

"As long as I deem necessary. You won't know how long. Only when it begins and when it is over."

"When it's over...Dona? How long...?"

For the first time, Lucifer hesitated. "The soul has no memory of its mate after Hell. Not at first. You won't remember her. Not for a long time."

It was an effort like lifting the weight of the world, but he put one foot back beneath him, then the other. Stood up. "We'll still be soul mates?"

"It may be many lives before you recognize her as such. But, yes."

*Surely time could be folded here, a thousand years to one minute on Earth. Science fiction couldn't be that far off from the truth.*

As Lucifer considered him, Nathan knew that the Being wasn't likely to respond well to such a persuasion. He thought hard, aching, needing her now. "May I keep her marks?" He directed his gaze to his piercings. "Can I have the compulsion to put them on myself when I'm older? To help me remember her?"

"It will not help."

"So what's the harm?"

He felt a blast of heat and sulfur that made his knees tremble. He locked them, tried to at least stay steady even if he couldn't meet the powerful Being's gaze.

"You're as stubborn as she is." Lucifer snorted. "Fine."

Pain could clarify as well as heal. Didn't a submissive know that better than anyone? Nathan tried to focus on what he knew instead of the fear, the realization he was about to do something which was far over his head, the knowledge of it reflected in those powerful eyes. What was important was what would best serve his Mistress. Bring him to her side more quickly. She needed him. The Lady had said so.

"So I'm guaranteed nothing." He said it without censure.

"Nothing, except the path itself." There was a hint of sympathy in Lucifer's voice. "That the journey continues until it's done."

"I'll know her." Nathan remembered that kiss, held it to him like his own beating heart. "She knows me. She looks at me and doesn't see a mirror. She sees me."

*She sees who I've been, who I am.*

More than that, more than the punishment or anything else, there was one thing that made him sure that he'd remember her.

She had faith in him, in who he could be. No one, not even himself, had ever given him that before. Since his brave, beautiful Mistress had never intended to have faith in a man again, that meant there had to be something worth loving in him. Had to be.

Everything flashed through his mind. When he got into the car. When he faced down the leopard. When he took all of Dona's punishments and yet still desired her. When he turned as he did now, to face that red glow and all the terrible things it represented.

*You're not weak… I have faith in you…*

"I'll know her anywhere, in any form. I won't lose her again. I won't lose myself again. She found me. She's my compass."

Lucifer inclined His head. "Noble sentiments. Are you strong enough to live up to them?"

Nathan began to move, the agony growing in his chest as he moved forward, as if the chasm returned all pains past and present. The pain of the piercings was suddenly there too, a gift. He didn't know if it came from Lucifer, the Lady, or Dona herself, but he held that particular pain to him like a promise. Not giving himself time to think, he broke into a run, moving toward that red glow, toward the promise of Dona that would wait on the other side. Toward his choice.

*Dona…*

He gave a fierce yell, defiant, let it echo out over the chasm and come back to him, blast him with heat. Gathering himself for the charge, he leaped out over the void.

Gravity snatched him, spinning him downward toward flames. As he fell, he could see the shadows upon shadows in the fire, waiting for him.

He had survived the abandonment of his mother, the cold hatred and indifference of his foster mothers. He'd killed a woman with his cruelty and taken away the hopes and dreams of countless others. Through some miracle, he'd gotten Dona as his soul mate. He'd found his only hope for salvation in Hell. The irony was not lost on him.

There was someone out there whose soul was connected to his. That meant he would never be alone, that someone needed him as much as he needed her. He could survive this. He would. He'd remember her. Or be damned to Hell forever, no matter where he ended up. His mouth opened on a scream as the fire swallowed him up, the shadows taking him eagerly.

\* \* \* \* \*

*Show mercy, love.*

"Did he show mercy to the women in his life, those he used to exorcise his own pain, futilely? How about Eliza? He must pay for his crimes, my lady. You would show mercy to all of them."

"I would." She looked fondly down at the image of the blue planet She held in Her palm, but there was sadness in Her gaze as well. *They make things so difficult for themselves.*

He reached out, for He couldn't bear Her sadness, and touched Her spirit. "It will all be well, my lady. He is strong, stronger than I first believed. The soul chooses its own justice, knows what it must pay to earn what it most desires. He will be all right."

"Perhaps we could choose a different way this time. Something that would be best for them both... After all, he is right. We can fold time, go back, change the way the world turns, rearrange the chess pieces...if it be for the highest good."

"You are a plague to me, my Lady."

"I love you, my dearest and only Lord."

187

# Chapter Twelve

### ℘

"Clear!"

Fire through his body, jerking him, his heart pumping irregularly, faltering, stopping again. *Oblivion. All I want is oblivion.*

"Again!"

Heart yelping in protest. *Don't make me feel... For one moment, don't make me feel...*

Air, painful, dragging into the lungs. Heart feeling like a jagged rock pounding on the inside of his chest. Fire in his midsection.

Light... Shattering agony, so bad that sound was coming from him... How could he hear his own screams when his vocal cords had been burned away an eternity ago along with all vestiges of a physical body? But yes, that was his voice. He was screaming, screaming the way a banshee screams. His eyes were squinting at the light, streaming with tears as he stared wildly around the room of people, things that he couldn't see clearly but fumbled to understand. Medical equipment, lights. He spoke words, he didn't know what, a wild stream of gibberish that turned the faces around him as white as their clothing. There was actually a moment they all stood back and he felt the weight of their wide-eyed stares even if he could not clearly see the features of their faces. Then he collapsed back on the gurney and the moment passed. They pounced back on him.

A haze as time churned forward. Lying somewhere, somewhere soft. Voices.

"You should have seen this guy in the ER...it was like we were transported to the set of *The Exorcist*. Scariest shit I've ever heard coming out of his mouth. His eyes…" Nathan felt a shudder run through the hand resting on the blood pressure cuff wrapped around his arm. "Colleen even fainted, if you can believe that. Man, nothing fazes that woman. We've had homeless people in here that acted way less crazy."

"Well, what did he say?"

"It wasn't what he said, it was how he said it… To be honest, I don't think anyone knows what he said. It was just…it sounds stupid, but it was like the room got cold as Alaska when he started screaming. For a minute we were all just frozen. I felt like I'd just found out my whole life was over, the worst feeling of despair and rage you've ever felt. You know how sometimes when you get so crazed by everything around you and you want to break out and you don't know how? You think up some crazy shit like shooting everyone? That was what this feeling was like."

"James, I think you've been on too many back-to-back shifts."

Trembling, shuddering, speaking words that he didn't remember… *The worst feeling of despair and rage you've ever felt.* That was probably as close to the truth as anything. Consigned to Hell, denied the ability to scream until he'd woken in a mortal body again.

He lost consciousness again, leaving the invisible James and his cohort behind. Moved through a thick fog where he had no sense of anything except he wasn't being hurt, tormented, burning or freezing. But he did ache. Deep inside him something ached, wanting to call out a name. He couldn't remember that name. That was the most horrible thing of all. He had to remember that name. Had to remember it…

For several days they kept him under heavy sedation, for he was so disoriented that everything frightened him. They told him his name and it meant nothing. He forgot it a moment later and had to ask again, mumble for it. They treated him with some impatience, which, compared to what he'd known, was akin to being given every consideration. As some cognizance returned, he noted one of his hands always remained handcuffed to the bedrail. He had a vague sense of a guard walking in and out at times, sitting outside the door. A prisoner. He'd always been a prisoner. The thought stretched his face in a grim smile. Having skin and a body...was strange. Perhaps he was free now, despite the handcuffs? He didn't want to be free. Needed that name. Need the name.

Then he'd doze and the nightmares would come back, nightmares even more powerful because he knew they weren't nightmares at all.

Fire...monsters...every fear that a person could imagine having. Those that lived in the darkest part of the psyche, things he hadn't even known he feared above all the other, more mundane fears, such as falling, being buried alive, spiders crawling across the skin to bite the most tender areas of the body, high-pitched shrieking laughter while being tortured, cold, darkness... No, there were worse fears. Shut in a small, dark place deep under the earth, being forgotten, unimportant for all eternity, tortured for amusement until the mind had shattered at the weight of all of it. Knowing that it was all deserved, so not even a sense of injustice provided a haven. There would be no escape from it, not ever.

He'd surrendered. Just surrendered, with no other choice. Standing free of all bonds, no longer even trying to draw away as everything was done to him and more. In the end, rationality fled, the mind, soul and body broken, nothing left. He couldn't remember the last time he'd thought of anything, a macabre meditative state based on torment instead of peace. His soul had floated, no longer weighed down by anything.

Then, lying on cold, wet stone, he'd felt a touch, a brief flash of eyes too powerful to be met, wings so pure white the beauty of them choked him.

*Goodbye, my child. You have paid for your sins. Now forgive yourself and love her as she deserves.*

*Don't fuck up.* That from a different presence, male. A brush of gray wings along his brow that offered encouragement with the warning.

A few days later, he remembered a conversation. Dr. Adams.

"Mr. Powell...can you understand me? You were stabbed in a fight at the prison. ...died for nine minutes before we restarted your heart. We think...Mr. Powell? Still with us? We think that may explain some of your disorientation and your memory problems..."

It was an understatement. At first, his vision was cloudy and he could only see blurry outlines of people or things. Everything startled him. Noise was too much. All of it could be the fire, monsters...

With his physical body, the attempt at rational thought returned. As he gained in strength, his mind tried to tell him that he'd had some weird hallucination when he was gutted in the knife fight, that none of it had been real.

No, it wasn't his mind trying to convince him of that. Not exactly. Jonathan. The part of him that would always be afraid of truth. But sometime during those minutes when he'd stood on the other side of the threshold between life and death, Nathan had taken the reins and Jonathan wasn't getting them back, no matter what he tried.

Nathan. That was what someone had called him, long ago when he was young and more possibilities had been open to him. Then later... Nathan and Jonathan. Two parts of the same whole. Made whole by someone... Someone...

It hurt so badly, the not knowing, that as he lay in bed on the tenth day he curled into himself and made the agony worse by putting the pressure of the position on the largest stab wound across his belly. He cupped his hand over it, held it as he rocked.

*I have to remember, I have to remember... It's not real. You're losing your fucking mind. There's no one. No one...*

191

*I love you, Nathan. I always will.*

He jerked up out of the bed and immediately bent double, cursing as the stitches tore and blood leaked onto his fingers. Looking down, he saw the blood drip and land on his bare groin, the skin of his cock. He had piercings. Why hadn't he noticed that before? Jesus Christ, piercings all over the place. Barbells up the bottom, a ring in the tip, a ring in his ball sac. His fingers touched the ladder, explored it, even as the blood wet his fingers and his genitals, mixing with the metal. A canvas of pain and memory, tormenting him as badly as his nightmares.

Her voice. He'd heard her voice. Who was she? His life depended on it, he was certain.

It was three months before he'd recovered enough mentally and physically to the satisfaction of the doctors to be released from the hospital. By then, he'd remembered who he was and why the police treated him with such hostility, doing the bare minimum for a prisoner who was in jail for aiding someone who'd tried to kill two cops. He found out he had six months left on his sentence.

Was it a dream? Was all of it some type of twisted retelling of *A Christmas Carol* to get him to change his ways? No and yes. Because that night *had* happened to Scrooge. It was a dream, but it was real as well.

*It's illusion and reality both…*

"Aarrgghhh…" Back in his cell, he snarled into his pillow, pressing his face against the scratchy surface. He wanted to beat his fists on the concrete walls until they were bloody to assuage this gnawing inside. "Who are you? *Who are you?*"

\* \* \* \* \*

He kept quiet, kept to himself during those six months. He began to write letters. Letters that he tore up and rewrote again and again, until he was regularly bartering for more packs of notebook paper. When he finally got one right, he'd carefully address it and put it on the shelf above his bunk, never mailing a single one, though the stack grew. It wasn't time to mail them. He didn't know how he knew that, just that it felt right. He was following his intuition. Lauren, Narcissa, Lady Jane... Even Mac Nighthorse.

His mother...then Eliza. The hardest one of all, a letter he would have to put on her grave because he had no ability to change what he'd done to the first person who'd ever truly loved him. He had to discard at least two versions because the tears he couldn't manfully control made the ink run and stain.

When he wasn't doing that, he did laundry duty or walked around the yard by himself. He paced by the portion of the fence that let him see the highway coming from the east. Keeping his eyes focused there the whole time, he felt like a tiger in a cage, waiting for release to go in that direction.

*A red car...a woman with dark hair...*

The other inmates gave him no more trouble. He didn't think to question it until Mario stated it baldly to him one day while they pulled laundry out of one of the carts. Mario was in for life and had been at the prison over twenty years.

"You got the 'Come to Jesus' look, the look of a man who know what Hell be like," he stated matter-of-factly. "The others don't want no part of that. Our boy Jonathan, he know what true fear is now."

"Nathan," he corrected automatically, and started folding.

Studying himself in the mirror in his cell, he saw it. A disturbing, haunting quality, something apparently so uncomfortable that many of the inmates never met his gaze now. In fact, most gave him a wide berth entirely.

That was fine, because nothing but that name he couldn't remember could ease the loneliness inside him. He couldn't face his own haunting expression for long either. It reminded him of too many things. Horrors that shifted in his mind like lingering shadows, too elusive to hold on to, but dogging him nevertheless. Particularly in his dreams, to the extent he slept as little as possible. He needed her healing touch...her love. Had he lost it? Or had he never had it, and he was making her up entirely, a hallucinatory side effect of his near-death experience, as the doctor suggested? Why couldn't he remember her name, otherwise?

But the only thing that gave him the courage to close his eyes at night was the occasional visit from her. She was worth any terror...

\* \* \* \* \*

He was on his knees, naked, in a room where the fire glowed warm and comforting, the heat sensual on the skin. Not searing or punishing. She was there, sitting in a wing-backed chair, her legs crossed, hands lying slim and graceful on the arms. She wore a short blue silk dress that clung to her breasts, showed him the high proud set of them, the points of her nipples. The indentation of her waist, flare of her hips, the line of her thigh. Her feet were bare. It was odd, the small toes painted a cherry red, curling into the carpet, when the rest of her looked so intimidating, so in control. Her sable hair waved around her face in a Twenties starlet type of way, accentuating those incredible lips. Her dark eyes seared his soul in a way that would make him gladly crack open his chest for her to brand it completely.

He had to approach her or he would simply die from the pain of not being near her. She granted his wish.

"Come here."

Moving forward on his knees, he kept his head down until he reached her feet. He groaned with relief when her fingers brushed his jaw, curved under his chin and lifted it so he could look into her face.

"I love you," he said. "I'll always love you. I'm so sorry."

Tears ran down his cheeks, over her fingers. Taking her hand to her mouth, she pressed the salt of him to her lips, keeping her eyes on him. Then she put her hands on his shoulders. "Lift me. Lay me down on the carpet and take off my clothes."

His hands trembled as he slid one arm around her back and scooted her forward to position the other hand under her knees. He picked her up. As he rose to his feet, he'd never felt anything as perfect as holding her in his arms, looking down into her face. Feeling her body relaxed, trusting his strength to hold her, take her where she commanded. Turning, he stepped before the fire and dropped to one knee to gently lay her down on the soft rug there. Her arms left his shoulders, drifting out to either side of her so she could grip the long strands of the carpet.

"Rough, Nathan. Take my dress off rough. I want to feel your power wash over me, knowing it's all mine to command."

It was a simple truth. All she had to do was say it and he would obey. It rose in him, savage and pure. He laid his hands on the neckline of that perfect, formfitting dress with its array of sparkles and rhinestones that followed the upper curves of her breasts and moved in a serpentine line around her hips. That design gave him a flash of some other memory, terrifying and arousing at once, gone before he could identify it. He didn't pause though, because his Mistress had ordered him to do something. Tearing the fabric from the point of the neckline to just below her mound, he found she was completely bare beneath it. She arched up when he froze, holding the fabric tightly in his fists. He stared down at her, the pink nipples, the delicate point of her bare sex, the graceful curves of her woman's body.

"Tear it all the way open."

He did, and now the dress spread out on either side of her, flaring out like a cape. When she lifted her slender white legs, her heels touched the small of his back, the upper curve of his buttocks. A soft, playful smile touched her lips as she exerted a slight, nudging pressure to bring him forward, angling up her hips with a mouthwatering display of flexibility.

"Inside me. Now."

Letting go of the dress, he laid hot, hungry hands on either side of those hips. Her fingers dug into the hard muscle of his biceps as he found her with his broad head. Slowly he pushed into wet heat, watching her undulate, her mouth open. Her breasts rose on a shuddering breath, her eyes sparkling with a passionate heat rivaling the fire. He knew if he could hold that gaze, he would never fear the touch of fire again. Not if this was the prize.

"Mistress."

"My name. Please, between us here and now, let me hear you say my name." She spread her thighs wider so he sank deeper.

"Oh, God...you feel..." Like heaven, heaven found in the depths of Hell.

"Nathan..." She was rippling, though he'd barely just entered her. As her muscles clamped on his cock, she dragged him down with her, making his vision gray, the grip of his hands become bruising as he sought to drive into her so deeply it would be like a fatal wound, keeping them linked through all eternity. Her throat was bared to him, pale, her tongue moist and pink as she opened her mouth on a scream.

"Dona..."

\* \* \* \* \*

*Dona.* His eyes sprang open, stared into the dark, wide awake. That was her name. It washed over him, everything coming in a jumble of images and thoughts that would take time to sort out, but she was real. He knew it now for sure, knew it the way he'd always known those nightmares were real, his literal trial by fire to earn her.

While identifying that name gave the gnawing fear within him an almost painful level of relief, she had another name. One he held on to, the name he called her in his soul.

*Mistress.*

It would make the nightmares and loneliness bearable. He would use it to remember that every action and every thought had to be with the intention of earning her love.

Reaching up in the darkness, he touched the letters, made sure they were still there.

*Please. I don't deserve her and I'll do what I have to do, but if I could only have her beside me while I do it, I won't ever take her for granted. I'll never doubt her love, never cause her pain...please, please, please... Give her back to me.*

*Dona. Mistress.* As he fell asleep again, the nightmares for once sullenly stayed in the shadows.

\* \* \* \* \*

"You're still moving like an eighty-year-old gimp." Jerry, the dayshift guard, made the observation as he processed his effects.

"Yeah, well, getting downed in a knife fight and dying for ten minutes will do that for you," Nathan responded dryly.

Today he would be released. All that quiet sense of waiting and tension that had been building in him like a coiled spring emanated from him like an engine revving. It got exponentially stronger as they put him through the checkout process, as he carefully bathed and shaved, dressed himself in his outside clothes he'd ordered for this day. A pair of tight jeans, a dark heavy cotton T-shirt, not so heavy that you couldn't see the bump of the nipple rings he wore. Most of the prisoners and the guards couldn't look at the piercings on his cock without wincing. They didn't hurt anymore, but if he barely touched himself there, he remembered her touch and became instantly erect from the sensation. For six months, he'd forced himself to wash without jacking off, despite his aching desire to do so. He wouldn't, not until she commanded it.

The movement as he walked rubbed the seam of his jeans over the piercings along his cock, carefully folded in his jeans with no underwear protecting it. His Mistress wouldn't want him wearing any underwear.

She would be here. He hoped. He wanted her to be with enough passion that it should be able to conjure her, if that was the way this worked. He hoped his prayers had earned him the chance to prove... Not that he could be worthy. He wasn't sure that was possible. But perhaps it wasn't a matter of being worthy. In his mind's eye he saw the stage again, the horrible moment of her greatest crime. He would love her, help her trust that a man could love her without betrayal. He would value the fragility of her heart far more than his own, because they were one. It was his heart. He wouldn't destroy their love with his fears. She wouldn't let him, for one thing. She knew what he was thinking before he thought it. She was the best woman to keep his ass on the right path. He'd make it his life's work to ensure she never regretted the effort. Or that Lucifer and His wondrous Lady didn't regret giving him this chance.

*If she'd just come for him.*

It was and wasn't a sense of déjà vu to step outside the prison gate, move to the edge of the highway. He had to cut through a parking lot, something that hadn't been there. There were buildings within view. A gas station about a quarter mile down the road to his right, a cluster of buildings that looked like farming structures to his right. More things that hadn't been there when he first met her. Trees, some green fields. As he stood there, squinting in the sun, his stomach hollow with anxiety, something caught his eye. Moving to the opposite side of the road, he bent and closed his hand on the cigarette lighter half covered in sand. A lighter that had been scratched with his initials on a bored night over a year ago.

She wasn't an illusion. He had faith in it. But finding the lighter helped. His fingers held it as his eyes shut. As the faint hum of an engine caught his ears, he hoped. He hoped.

He had served his time in more ways than one. Now he was free. Only he didn't want to be a free man. He wanted Dona's leash upon him, needed it.

Like a scientist, he'd made his mind a microscope, focusing in on the tiniest portions of her. The way she had turned her head. The curve of her lips. The pain lingering in her eyes.

*If it's just the bus and I have to get on it, I will. I'll keep going as long as I have to, to prove I deserve her. I will deliver every letter alone, face the karma I deserve. Live every life alone if I have to. I just...oh God, I don't know if I can survive another minute without her...*

He lifted his gaze to the horizon.

She was coming. The red Mercedes as he remembered it, her dark hair flying, only something was different this time. When she slowed, stopped alongside him, it was not with the dynamic fanfare, and Dona was wearing a... He blinked. A pale yellow sundress, as fresh and feminine as a lily. Her feet against the pedals were bare, a pair of canvas sneakers pushed just beneath the seat. The Goth makeup was gone. As he reached out, removed her sunglasses with trembling fingers, there were just the dark beautiful eyes seeking his. Real, alive. His Mistress, but a Mistress of Hell no longer. Mortal, like he was.

She had accepted that she might face pain again, but that it was time for her to rejoin the world. She'd had the faith to risk her heart again, to believe that he would provide the love that would make that risk worth it. He found he couldn't speak at the enormity of that gift. Behind the anticipation of seeing him, he could see she was as scared as he was.

"So..." Her voice was soft as he cupped her cheek, his thumb tracing her lips. They quivered as she pressed her face against his touch, her gaze never leaving his face. "You're sure about this? It's a hard road, this life. You have a lot of debts to pay."

What he wanted to do was hold her, tell her he wouldn't let her down. She was tough as nails, but she'd come this way at a cost. It was a miracle.

He'd never thought of himself as deserving a miracle, but maybe that's why they were called miracles. To give the undeserving a chance to change.

*Thank you.*

"It's the reality in which I get you. That's all that matters to me."

At her expression, he couldn't wait any longer. He slid his hand to the back of her neck and half lifted her out of the car, his other hand going around her waist to crush her to him as he covered her mouth with his. He drank her in like a man dying of thirst in the desert under the cruel sun. Surrounded by fire, she was his salvation and damnation, and he'd accept both to hold on to her.

When they parted, her eyes were closed. He touched her lips with his thumb again and her mouth curved at last, even as he caught one of her tears on his fingertip. She dropped her head back, pinned him with her gaze.

Though the dress was innocent, that smile was not. "Then get your ass in this car. Your Mistress has plans for it. I want those jeans open. In case I want to play with the only stick this car has."

With a rakish grin, he kissed her hand, held on to it as long as he could before he had to release it to circle to the passenger side. When he got to the car door, he backed a step away and vaulted over it. He landed with a bounce in the passenger seat, despite the agonizing twinge to his midsection.

It was only pain. He wasn't afraid to experience pain to please his Mistress. In fact, he was looking forward to it.

# Epilogue
## *Six months later*

&)

"So *this* was a success?"

Dona applied the ice pack gently to Nathan's swelling left eye, cupping his chin in her free hand. She couldn't help a quick stroke of the feathered eyebrow, needing to feel the soft skin that creased at the corner of his unmarked blue eye at her amused question.

"Well, considering she could have just shot me as a trespasser and dragged my body into the house…"

Lifting his hands to her wrists, he curled his fingers around them, not impeding her, just caressing. He did that a lot, touched small portions of her anatomy as if he was savoring, memorizing, always seemingly awed at the gift of being able to touch her. Even though they'd touched each other so many ways since he'd been released from prison, often with more raw need than reverence. But maybe they were the same thing.

When she bent, pressed her lips against his swollen upper one, she knew no matter how he touched her, her body responded. Whether it was the most casual brush of contact when they walked down the street hand in hand at night, exchanging quips with the street vendors, or far more intimate couplings in their tiny apartment.

"You could have worked up to them," she murmured against his mouth. "In Violet's mind, you almost got her husband killed. It might have been best to wait another five years. Maybe until the end of the next decade."

He dipped his head, brushing her cheek with his soft hair as he pressed a kiss into her palm. Glancing at her beneath

201

those long lashes, he worked up her wrist to the pulse point there, his tongue teasing it to a faster cadence.

"Be still," she reproved. "I'm trying to be a doctor here."

He lingered, tracing a line back down her palm that caused a stir in her lower extremities. The playful desire in his eyes goaded her. When she curled her hand, pricking his face with her nails, he obeyed and released her. Her good slave— but never too good.

"I wanted... I've been thinking about them a lot. She wouldn't let me in the house, said my filth wasn't going to infect her home. I think they have a kid now. There was this little bike with training wheels by the front door."

He rose, moved into the bathroom and pulled off his shirt, wetting a cloth to run down his arms. Dona made herself stay where she was, watching him remove some of the dirt he'd accumulated from his day's work.

She quelled the desire to reach out, soothe the pain. His heart had changed, so it was difficult for her to let him do what he needed to do. But he never faltered. Never asked for pity. Only that she be there when he got done doing it.

"It may not have been personal. She may have been referring to how dirty you were from work."

He met her gaze in the mirror, a rueful smile crossing his firm lips at her attempt to tease, but he lifted his shoulder in an apparent casual shrug as he bent his attention to the cloth, wiped it across his bare chest. She liked him smooth, had him keep himself shaved for her, though she'd had him keep the hair on his head the way it was now, the shoulder length that let her see all the different color variations from the sun.

"They've seen me cleaned up. All shellacked. I wanted them to see me. Who I am. This is who I am."

All the potentials of strength and intelligence she knew he possessed were emerging. This handsome, magnificent man was slowly becoming as complex and beautiful inside as out. He took her breath away, on many different levels.

Despite herself, she moved to the opening of the small bathroom, reached out and ran her fingers down the center of his back.

"So what happened? Use the other clean cloth for your face. The coolness will feel good."

He complied, so his next words came out from behind terrycloth. It also served as a blindfold, helping him to get the words out, as she knew it would.

"I told her I would respect her wishes, but I needed to speak to Mac, and to her. They listened." There was wonder in his voice. A quiet triumph, laced with contentment and acceptance. "When it was over, she didn't say anything to me, just walked into the house. But Mac stood there and looked at me awhile, then asked me if I wanted a beer. We sat out on their dock for about a half hour, drinking beer, not saying much. Then he shook my hand, wished me luck. I saw her watching me as I walked back down the street to catch the bus. She didn't look...she looked like she was thinking, not hating."

Dona stroked her knuckles down the valley of his spine. She knew what it was to love a man with her whole self. She'd dared to do it twice now, and this second time she knew she'd do anything for him. She couldn't say she didn't understand Violet's anger. The black eye she'd given him the moment he'd stepped onto her property, the follow-up punch to the jaw.

But it hurt, imagining how Nathan would have stood there, taking the blows, a man big and strong enough to stand toe to toe with scarier things than a pissed-off woman who was barely over five feet tall, even if she was a cop. He would have waited until she finished, the blood filling his mouth. Then once again, he'd quietly ask for a chance to talk to them. It was that which would have gotten through to Violet. Seeing that there was something different about him. Something worth hearing.

He was fiercely devoted to the quest to make amends. Fiercely devoted to taking care of Dona. Maybe too devoted, she reflected.

She worked late hours at the free clinic. While society's memory of the previous life associated with her name had vanished, her medical degree and credentials were unquestioned. The advantage of having Lucifer as her previous employer, she suspected. Another of the quietly amazing gifts she'd been given.

Every day, Nathan came to escort her home, no matter how tired he was after a hard and hot day of roofing in the new subdivisions going up on the outskirts of the city.

"A kick-ass Mistress you might be," he'd tease her, "but you're still a woman. My woman. You're not walking home alone."

He liked to hold her hand as they walked. They'd talk about their day, watch the neighborhood kids squeeze in that last moment of play in the darkening streets.

Those moments of male testosterone meshed oddly well with his submission to her in the bedroom, his willingness to serve her however she desired. But it wasn't just the roughness of the neighborhood. He knew how she felt about opening the door of their home alone, fighting the hold of what might be behind it, a lingering phobia.

Therefore, when she woke to find herself held tightly by him in the loneliest hours of the night, she understood. He'd tear open his heart and let her have it if she asked. It was all for her. He'd found something worth saving his soul *for*, and that had made all the difference. She wondered if he understood he'd saved her soul as well.

"I want to celebrate." He turned suddenly and caught her about the waist, twirling her, sending the handful of cotton balls she held flying and making her laugh with his boyish exuberance. The light and the shadows in her mind joined hands, making it the best kind of ache to look up at him. "I got paid yesterday. I'm taking you out to dinner and for ice cream afterward."

She cocked a brow. "*And* ice cream?"

"Waffle cone, cookie crumb topping, everything." Sobering, he brought her closer. Despite the injuries to his face, she got lost looking into his blue eyes, feeling the muscled length of his body press against her. "Anything you want, Mistress. Today, tomorrow…"

She let him kiss her, and as he deepened it, those calloused hands clutched her hips, pulled her closer in male demand. She decided she was going to exercise a Mistress's prerogative. Dinner could wait. Ice cream and him. Those were the only two things she needed, and if she could have them together, so much the better. She had half a pint of mocha vanilla swirl still in the freezer. The microwave would melt it just enough…

* * * * *

A summer breeze flitted through the curtains. The bed was stripped down to just sheets as his body stretched over her, giving her the pleasure of running her palms up his strong arms, braced on either side of her. Across the broadness of his back, down to his hips, slightly sticky from the ice cream she'd licked off his buttocks and his long cock. He'd had some too, and her pussy still ached from the pleasure of the cold and heat mixed, the warmth of his mouth before she'd had him replace it with his cock.

Lean, a roofer's spare body, but all muscled and more wide-shouldered than expected. When he bent to her, catching her lips in a kiss that was somewhat off center because of the rhythm of his body stroking into hers, everything was dusky, dim, soft at the edges in the quiet room. The noises of the street outside blended with the radio inside.

"Dona." He murmured her name, sinking deeper. She arched, wanting all of him and more.

"Mine," she whispered back, biting his lips a little harder, feeling him swell inside her at the sensual punishment, the claim on him.

"Yours," he agreed. "Forever, Mistress. Yours to fuck...however, whenever..." Humor glinted through his gaze, but something even more intense.

"Mine to love."

"Yours to love." He bent, kissed the point of her sternum, just beneath her breasts. "Yours to keep."

Her protector. Her lover.

Each declaration in her mind was punctuated by his next kiss as he worked his way up the bone that helped guard her heart. But she didn't need anything to guard her heart anymore.

This quiet moment held all the answers. He had her. She had him. Happiness was as simple as this. As she opened herself further to him, his arms tightened around her. She let herself be absorbed by him, her slave. The man who called her Mistress.

The man who had her heart because he believed in what lay behind redemption, forgiveness, karma, Eden... What was worth every torment. He'd helped her believe in it again as well, giving her the strength to follow him out of Hell and link her destiny to life again. To him.

Love and faith. Inseparable, because they were One.

Just like soul mates.

## The End

# Also by Joey W. Hill

∞

# About the Author

శు

I've always had an aversion to reading, watching or hearing interviews of favorite actors, authors, or musicians because so often you find that the real person does not measure up to the beauty of the art they produce. You find their politics or religion distasteful, or you find they're shallow and self-absorbed, or a vacuous mophead without a lick of sense. And from then on, though you still may appreciate their craft or art, it has somehow been tarnished. Therefore, whenever I'm asked to provide personal information about myself for readers, a ball of anxiety forms in my stomach as I think, "Okay, the next couple of paragraphs can change forever the way someone views my stories." Why on earth does a reader want to know about me? It's the story that's important.

So here it is. I've been given more blessings in my life than any one person has a right to have. Despite that, I'm a Type A, borderline obsessive-compulsive paranoiac who worries that I will never live up to expectations. I've got more phobias than anyone (including myself) has patience to read about. I can't stand talking on the phone, I dread social commitments, and the idea of living in monastic solitude with my husband, a few animals, books and writing is as close an idea to paradise as I can imagine. I love chocolate, but with that deeply ingrained, irrational female belief that weight equals worth, I manage to keep it down to a minor addiction. I adore good movies. I'm told I work too much. Every day is spent trying to get through the never ending "to do" list to snatch a few minutes to write.

This is because, despite all these mediocre and typical qualities, for some miraculous reason, these wonderful characters well up out of my soul with stories to tell. When I manage to find enough time to write, sufficient enough that the precious "stillness" required rises up and calms all the competing voices in my head, I can step into their lives, hear what these characters are saying, what they're feeling, and put it down on paper. It's a magic beyond description, akin to truly believing that my husband loves me, winning the trust of an animal who has known only fear or apathy, making a true connection with someone else, or knowing for certain that I've given a reader a moment of magic through those written words. It's a magic that reassures me that there is Someone, far wiser than myself, who knows the permanent path to that garden of stillness, where there is only love, acceptance and a pen waiting for hours and hours of uninterrupted, blissful use.

If only I could finish that darned "to do" list.


Joey welcomes comments from readers. You can find her website and email address on her author bio page at www.ellorascave.com.


### Tell Us What You Think

We appreciate hearing reader opinions about our books. You can email us at Comments@EllorasCave.com.

# Why an electronic book?

We live in the Information Age—an exciting time in the history of human civilization, in which technology rules supreme and continues to progress in leaps and bounds every minute of every day. For a multitude of reasons, more and more avid literary fans are opting to purchase e-books instead of paper books. The question from those not yet initiated into the world of electronic reading is simply: *Why?*

1.  *Price.* An electronic title at Ellora's Cave Publishing and Cerridwen Press runs anywhere from 40% to 75% less than the cover price of the exact same title in paperback format. Why? Basic mathematics and cost. It is less expensive to publish an e-book (no paper and printing, no warehousing and shipping) than it is to publish a paperback, so the savings are passed along to the consumer.

2.  *Space.* Running out of room in your house for your books? That is one worry you will never have with electronic books. For a low one-time cost, you can purchase a handheld device specifically designed for e-reading. Many e-readers have large, convenient screens for viewing. Better yet, hundreds of titles can be stored within your new library—on a single microchip. There are a variety of e-readers from different manufacturers. You can also read e-books on your PC or laptop computer. (Please note that Ellora's Cave does not endorse any specific brands.

You can check our websites at www.ellorascave.com or www.cerridwenpress.com for information we make available to new consumers.)

3. *Mobility.* Because your new e-library consists of only a microchip within a small, easily transportable e-reader, your entire cache of books can be taken with you wherever you go.

4. *Personal Viewing Preferences.* Are the words you are currently reading too small? Too large? Too... ANNOYING? Paperback books cannot be modified according to personal preferences, but e-books can.

5. *Instant Gratification.* Is it the middle of the night and all the bookstores near you are closed? Are you tired of waiting days, sometimes weeks, for bookstores to ship the novels you bought? Ellora's Cave Publishing sells instantaneous downloads twenty-four hours a day, seven days a week, every day of the year. Our webstore is never closed. Our e-book delivery system is 100% automated, meaning your order is filled as soon as you pay for it.

Those are a few of the top reasons why electronic books are replacing paperbacks for many avid readers.

As always, Ellora's Cave and Cerridwen Press welcome your questions and comments. We invite you to email us at Comments@ellorascave.com or write to us directly at Ellora's Cave Publishing Inc., 1056 Home Avenue, Akron, OH 44310-3502.

erridwen, the Celtic Goddess of wisdom, was the muse who brought inspiration to storytellers and those in the creative arts. Cerridwen Press encompasses the best and most innovative stories in all genres of today's fiction. Visit our site and discover the newest titles by talented authors who still get inspired - much like the ancient storytellers did, once upon a time.

## CERRIDWEN PRESS

www.cerridwenpress.com

*Discover for yourself why readers can't get enough of the multiple award-winning publisher*

*Ellora's Cave.*

*Whether you prefer e-books or paperbacks,*

*be sure to visit EC on the web at*
*www.ellorascave.com*

*for an erotic reading experience that will leave you breathless.*

LaVergne, TN USA
20 March 2011
220878LV00002B/106/P